DELUMI

Howard Reede-Pelling

Order this book online at www.trafford.com
or email orders@trafford.com

Most Trafford titles are also available at major online book retailers.

Printed in the United States of America.

ISBN: 978-1-4269-5223-4 (sc)
ISBN: 978-1-4269-5225-8 (e)

Library of Congress Control Number: 2010919285

Trafford rev. 12/25/2010

North America & international
toll-free: 1 888 232 4444 (USA & Canada)
phone: 250 383 6864 • fax: 812 355 4082

CONTENTS

PREFACE

Delumi is the story of a female managing director of a large Investment Company. Delumi Vido and her boss get into strife crossing the Nullabour and their limousine crashes. Her boss is killed in that accident and Delumi is lost in the desert.

This is the story of how she manages to survive the desert with the help of an Aborigine community and becomes the flagship of the company. Many adverse events are put in her way but she overcomes them and the Investment Company flourishes.

All characters in this fictional tale are entirely made up and no reference is willingly made to persons alive or deceased. This book remains the property of Howard Reede-Pelling, the Author. No part or portion of it may be used without the Authority of the publisher or the Author.

Chapter One

ORDEAL

Delumi Vido raised a weary arm to wipe the globules of perspiration from her dripping brow, hoping to ease the stinging of the rivulets affecting her vision. With shaded eyes the young lady earnestly scanned the arid, far horizon. Nothing! No movement stirred within the wide vista of her roving gaze. One or two stunted trees every kilometre or so for as far as she could distinguish through her tear-streaked, glazed red eyes, irritated by hours of plodding through this inhospitable, dry and dusty sand blown land-scape; was all that could be discerned. A stark, dying tree afforded scant shade from the fierce burning rays of the merciless sun. Delumi collapsed as a discarded sack of potatoes into the meagre shade. Despair and hopelessness etched deep into her worried face; a face which glistened with beauty and grace albeit though tear-stained and grimy. The clothes she wore, once elegant and neat, now were as a dishevelled bunch of torn and dirty rags. The ravages of time, distance and the fight for survival had transformed the once clean and trim young executive into a quite pitiful, ragged tramp. Delumi heaved a weary sigh and fell asleep. Again in sleep, she re-lived the most frightening prelude to her present dilemma. With her wealthy industrialist employer, Thurston Klotz, they had been driving across the Nullabour Plains of Western Australia to settle the terms of a lucrative contract at an isolated mining lease. They opted for the overland drive in preference to the company twin-engines jet by way of a diversion from the monotony of the continual flying business trips. As Thurston had quoted "A change is as good as a holiday!" This was not the holiday either of the travellers had in mind. Whilst Delumi shuffled through papers and re-checked the wording of contracts, Thurston drove the company limousine; the usual driver having been offered a week off. It was while Thurston's attention was diverted to a particular paragraph queried by Delumi, that a kangaroo resting in the shade of some scrub became agitated by the fast approaching vehicle and suddenly bounded out in front of it. Thurston valiantly attempted to avoid the marsupial and in doing so, caused the long limousine to slew sideways. A large boulder by the roadside straightened the careening limo' with a severe jolt and Thurston's head crashed against the door upright, sharply snapping his neck. He died instantly; a foot jammed the accelerator to the floor. The ungainly limousine sped out of control pitching and tossing across the Nullabour; Delumi unconscious in her seatbelt, having also bumped her head. The vehicle sped uncontrolled for many kilometres across the rough and rocky terrain, miraculously missing trees but occasionally grubbing saltbushes as it bolted aimlessly. Eventually a ditch rolled the limousine; Delumi was jolted awake by the exploding gas tanks. Otherwise unhurt, the very bewildered young lady released her restraining seat-belt and hurriedly, frantically, quit the blazing wreck to scurry in terrified bounds for the safety of a large rocky outcrop. In awe, she watched the remains of the vehicle and her employer, as they burned! For three days Delumi searched in vain for the road over which the two had been travelling, but city-bred, she had no idea of bush craft or direction and had stumbled in abject terror in any but the right direction. Without food or water the young body was beginning to dehydrate. Mirages began flashing with scintillating realism before her tired and flickering vision; her spirit and strength, fast declining. In sleep she twitched and rolled from the blessed shade into the hot sand and searing sunlight. Delumi roused and forced her tired being back into the meagre shade. After an hour of rest another effort was made and the hopeless young lady struggled to her feet. She scanned the horizons again and finding no comfort in that effort, boldly plodded forth. Two more kilometres of trudging found her beside a larger shrub of the desert than hitherto had come her way. As Delumi tried to crawl under it into the comfort of the shade, her head swam dizzily and she fainted; falling prone into the welcome safety of the darker shadows of the shrub. Warm liquid trickling over her lips woke Delumi. She opened her eyes to the spectacle of a grinning black face, which displayed huge white teeth. A comical yet strangely cultured voice addressed her. "Ay, Missus! You a long way from somewhere, I reckon!" Delumi opened her mouth to speak but no sound came forth; more water was squeezed into it. The aborigine broke another small branch from the shrub and began pounding it with a rock. The girl watched in awe as this stupid man wasted his energy trying to kill a dead stick. She mentally apologised as the 'stupid man' squeezed the pulp to let more droplets of water into her parched mouth. Delumi fervently swallowed and licked the while she attempted to smile her thanks. Having recovered slightly and with a not so parched throat, Delumi struggled to a sitting position. "Thank you!" She croaked. The huge grin again engulfed the handsome black features. "Ay Missus. Reckon you can walk a little bit over there?" He pointed to the West but Delumi did not know that. "Plenty water in the rocks. Come Missus, try!" The youth gently raised the weak girl to her feet. She marvelled at his strength for such a slightly built lad. Together they made their way in the direction indicated, the aborigine bearing the brunt of the burden at first. As they progressed, Delumi found her strength returning slightly and was able to carry her own weight a little better. A rocky outcropping came into sight. It was little more than a small wall and no creek or billabong could be discerned. Delumi began to fear that the intended water supply which they were seeking may very well have dried up; her face fell. Her guide led the frail girl to a ledge and bade her sit. He then reached into a crevice with both hands cupped and withdrew them brimming with water – the water of life! Delumi fairly charged at the precious liquid spilling a little in her frenzied fervour. "Easy Missus!" Her host chided. "Plenty more – ay?" The girl nudged him away and helped herself. After six or seven cupped hands full of water were dispatched, the aborigine pulled Delumi away with a caution. "No more yet – wait – waste not good!" He took a few hands full himself, then filled a small leather pouch from his waist-string, to tide them over the next stage of their journey. Feeling more refreshed and with renewed hope, Delumi studied her stalwart saviour. He was but a youth, possibly seventeen or eighteen. Clad only in a loin-cloth and a head band which held up unruly black locks. He was barefooted and had a working boomerang through the 'g' string at his back. A wooden sliver with what appeared to be a very sharp edge was also thrust through the 'g' string. Delumi wondered how often that 'knife' cut through the supporting string and then she smiled that such a strange thought should come to her. The youth also carried a very long spear.

"Wallaballagalla!" The youth spoke. Delumi looked puzzled.

"Pardon?" She asked.

"Wallaballagalla – ay! It's me name, just call me Wally!"

"Oh! Er – Delumi, Delumi Vido! Please call me Delumi!" She smiled coyly.

A huge grin which seemed ever to live upon the face of this welcome young man was again evident.

"Delumi?" He sounded the name with fluency.

"Crikey! You white ones got real funny names – ay?"

Delumi smiled again, her cracked face paining under the wind and sun burn.

"Thank you for finding me. Where do we go from here and how far it to get anywhere – anywhere at all has to be better than here?"

"No worries Missus. A couple of days and we get to my uncle's place!" Wally settled Delumi down under another shady bush, then told her to stay put and wait – he would go and get some tucker! As he silently disappeared, Delumi pondered the next phase of this terrible excursion. Uncle's place would probably be just a humpy further out into this damnable desert. She did not look forwards with very great expectations. Wally returned with a quite large but scrawny lizard and some tubers. Delumi could imagine him finding and catching the lizard but where on earth in this dust-ridden hell-hole he managed to find tubers, was beyond her. She just shook her head in disbelief and watched as the lad built a fire and threw the carcass of the lizard upon it. No butchering, no skinning or preparing, no gutting – just a whole lizard to sizzle on the embers. Wally passed a few tubers to Delumi as he lustily chewed upon some himself.

"Put 'im to good use Missus!" He said. After having turned the lizard once or twice, Wally declared the meat ready. It was not unlike tearing a cooked chicken apart with a remarkably similar taste. Delumi raised her eyebrows in pleasant surprise.

"Good tucker, ay?" Wally grinned his toothy grin.

Having dispatched their meal and all traces of the fire covered with sand, the pair ventured forth

"Walkabout now when the sun is down and into the evening, we travel better, hot sunny day no good for walk. We rest in the day, make better travel!" Wally explained. Delumi nodded. She realised the young man knew what he was doing and was experienced at it, she also realised how hopeless and very helpless she was in this environment. It was most comforting to have someone else shoulder all the responsibility for a change. Young though her escort was, Delumi relished the respite from her heavy workload and felt quite confident in putting her future and faith in this resourceful aborigine, named 'Wally'. After three hours of steady walking, Wally declared it was time to rest. They sat close together against a rock which kept the very slight breeze off them. The evening was becoming quite cool as it always does upon the desert at night. Wally stretched his legs out and packed dirt all over them.

"Keeps 'em warm, Missus!" He explained. Delumi did likewise. They slept for a further few hours. Delumi was awakened by Wally rising.

"Time to go Missus!" He stated.

"Getting' too cold just sitting. Lookit 'im the moon – he's a big fella – ay? Walk now and get warm, sleep in tomorrow's hot!" Once again they shuffled off.

Another very hot day began to draw to a close. The pair had covered a remarkably long distance during the evening and then the early morning, they rested through the heat of another day. Now it was time to get moving again, this was only possible for Delumi through the expertise of Wally. This young man timed their walks and rest periods to perfection, conserving energy so well that Delumi actually began to recover from the terrifying ordeals of her first three days alone. Water was still a very scarce commodity and was used sparingly, even though Wally seemed to have unlimited knowledge of supply areas. Food was not all that easy to come by; however, the pair was never really hungry. Another lizard and more tubers found beneath a rocky outcropping at one of the watering places, sufficed to give the nourishment needed to keep going.

"Soon be there Missus!" Wally stated, as he pointed ahead.

In the far distance Delumi could barely recognise what appeared to be a homestead. Fears of Wally's uncle living in a humpy, abated.

"Is that cattle I see, Wally?" Delumi asked.

"Too right!" Wally grinned his toothy grin. "It's me uncle's place – he runs a cattle station!" Delumi looked her amazement.

"But I thought only white folk ran cattle stations?"

"Nah!" Wally became enthusiastic. "Maybe in them dark day's way back – now the people of the earth manage their own affairs – like they always did. The Ballagalla tribes have grown from this land since time began; they are the land around here!"

Because of the flat nature of the terrain, the house forever seemed to be far away. The two continued for two more hours before they got anywhere near the buildings. Cattle were roaming more thickly about as Wally and Delumi finally came to the outer boundary of the homestead yards proper. A utility left the house and came their way. Wally sat on a rock awaited it. "Sit down Missus, they coming to get us!" The weary young body needed no second bidding; she also sat and watched the dusty approach of the vehicle. There was but one person in the cabin, the driver. He was a very large aborigine not unlike Wally in looks but five or so years older. In the back of the utility were half a dozen noisy, chattering youngsters. As the vehicle stopped, all alighted and upon noticing the white girl, the children became silent. Not so the driver, he warmly slapped his cousin on the back; dislodging much dust.

"Ay Wal!" He grinned, looking keenly in surprise at Delumi. "We expected a wallaby as a gift – we don't eat whites no more!" Delumi started with a gasp, fear crossed her features.

Wally eased her trauma.

"Ah – take no notice of him Missus – he's only funnin'!"

The driver courteously held out his hand to Delumi.

"Wal's me cousin – we haven't seen him since last summer – I'm Johnny. My dad owns this cattle station. Hop in the ute and we'll get back home for a cool drink an' some tucker!"

Delumi prettily thanked him and introduced herself. As the group motored back to the homestead, the children jabbered on in their own tribal tongue in the back.

"What you doin' dragging a white lady 'round the desert, Wal?" Johnny asked.

"I was lying almost dead under a bush when Wally found me – thank goodness – he has been marvellous! Thank you so much Wally!" Delumi answered for him. Johnny nodded, and then said.

"Nah! There's more to it than that – how did you know she was there Wal?"

"Yeah!" Wally explained. "On me way here I saw the smoke of the burning car and went to have a look-see. Found the driver an' I buried 'im beside the wreck, then scouted about and found the Missus' footprints; so I followed them – thassall!"

"Oh! Wally – thank you – oh, thank you so very much!" Delumi pressed his arm.

"Yeah! Sorry about your husband, couldn't do much but bury 'im!" Wally was not grinning. Delumi was quick to explain.

"No – he – he wasn't my husband Wally, he was my boss! His name was Thurston Klotz. We were on our way to the mine when we crashed!"

"The gold mine?" Johnny asked. When Delumi nodded, Wally said.

"Lots of our people work there, mostly drivin' the heavy machinery. Our people don't go down under too much, we got too many dreamin's!"

"We were due at the mine a week ago, they must be wondering what has happened to us!" Delumi worried.

"Don't worry – we got communications at the house – you can make some calls from there!" Johnny assured her, then as an afterthought. "Ay! Your boss wouldn't be from some doin's called 'K.H.I.L.', would he?"

"Why yes!" Delumi turned to him in surprise. "He WAS Klotz Holdings and Investments Limited!" Johnny nodded.

"There was something on the telly news about him and his Business Manager going missing. It reckoned they've disappeared without a trace, been searchin' for days. Guess they will be glad to hear from you; I reckon!"

As the 'entourage' arrived at the station proper amid billowing clouds of choking red dust and the horde of dis-embarking, noisy youngsters; a group of people emerged from the house to welcome them. The most imposing of these was Johnny's father and tribal elder; the owner of the cattle station. He was indeed a striking person. Dressed in denim waist-jacket and jeans, with a rather battered wide brimmed Akubra hat firmly jammed upon his greying shock of loose black hair; which contrasted oddly to a flowing white beard almost reaching to his heavily buckled belt. Either side of him was a large plump lady who proved to be Johnny's mother and a short grizzled old-timer who was the head man of the Ballagalla tribe. Delumi of a sudden realised that she must present a wretched sight, dusty and bedraggled as she was; far removed from the most meticulously dressed and groomed person who set out on this ill-fated trip.

Chapter Two

RE-ORGANIZING

"G'day Wallaballagalla!" The big man boomed, upon recognising his brother's youngest son.

"Where did you find this one?" He strode forwards with outstretched hand. "I'm Djindagarra – call me Djinda! Come on in outa the hot – crikey – you look like you had a rough time!"

He smiled hugely at Delumi as he politely took her hand to help her up the steps of the verandah; then turned to her escort. "Hey Wal! Fancy makin' a white one travel walkabout – ain't you still got that motorbike?" Wally grinned.

"Ay! That dopey machine – it don't like rocks – buckled the front bit, so I just left 'er there, ay?"

After introductions and a most welcome cool drink, Delumi was taken to spruce herself up a bit by the matriarch of the household. Manny Binnagalla fussed over Delumi, much in the manner depicted in the movies of the Negro slave peoples of the Texas Deep South, perhaps relishing in a new female about the property to help divert the sameness of every-day existence in this far out-flung community. And a community it certainly was. As the Australian aborigine is heavily steeped in tribal custom, family tradition and togetherness; this particular house-hold was a very large community indeed! There were numerous out-houses and many lean-to's scattered in and about the home paddock – if it could even faintly be likened to a paddock at all – more in keeping with a dust bowl, so scarce was any sign of grass. Lean cattle dogs were in abundance as were the well-fed children of the tribe; playing various games with sticks and small spears. Some of the older folk were in small groups talking and showing a keen interest at the advent of a white girl in their domain. Delumi's most urgent interest was the radio-phone. She was allowed privacy to make her calls to head office and home, to assure all that she was safe and to report the sad demise of Thurston Klotz! Her private Cessna would be flown in at first light the very next day, there were now urgent loose ends to attend and new arrangements to be made for the continuity of the Klotz empire. Delumi also ordered her personal secretary to bring some changes of clothing and face-saving cosmetics. A special delivery was also ordered. The vagabond appearance did not ride well on the personality of such a vibrant young executive. Her wardrobe could not arrive quickly enough. The cattle station boasted an abundance of water, for there was a water-table of immense proportions beneath the property and extending to the east for seventy to one hundred kilometres. Three windmills pumped the pure clear water. One to the main house, the corral area and another one far out in the pastures provided for the stock needs. To the west were the mining company and the hundreds of square kilometres of land over which the Klotz Holdings and Investment Limited were negotiating a lease. Gold bearing ore was proven to exist to the east of the hills north of the present mine and that was two hundred kilometres west of the cattle station and possibly land belonging to the Ballagalla peoples.

A refreshing shower and a change of clothing kindly loaned by one of Djinda's pretty daughters, gave Delumi a new lease on life. She was resplendent as she sat and enjoyed her first meal for more than a week, with her wonderful hosts. A flicker of a smile crossed her face as she glanced about the table and noticed the wall of black faces with flashing white teeth. Reminiscent of a Minstrel Show, she thought; then mentally apologised to her hosts.

"Ay! You fit in well Missus!" Wally's face lit up. "You got 'im one big laugh on your face jus' like us Ballagalla fellers!"

A touch of colour tinted her cheeks as Delumi stammered. "Oh! I - I'm sorry. I just felt all strange and out of place here and it struck me as funny!" Djinda boomed out.

"No one is out of place here Miss Delumi. Anybody who eats with us is one of us and welcome!"

"Oh please do not be so formal – no Miss, no Missus – please just call me Delumi. I will fit in better then and thank you so much for making me welcome and for all of your assistance!"

The meal was a happy riot for Delumi, as the younger generations of the house were truly a fun-loving group and she warmed to their shameless banter and frivolity. It did have some bounds however, as the more senior elders often gave serious looks or a quickly pointed finger, if the teenagers got too bold in front of a guest. One small girl standing in a doorway, with finger in mouth, was coyly watching Delumi with wide black eyes. Delumi smiled at her and the youngster quickly pulled out of sight. After having eaten, Delumi attempted to help clear the table. The men folk let her but the women in the kitchen took the plates and bowls from her, saying that there were too many in the kitchen anyway. Delumi was a guest and should not do the cleaning. She sat on the verandah. The shy little girl stood in the doorway again, quietly appraising the white lady. Delumi smiled at the girl and beckoned her over. The little girl slowly shook her head. Balla Ballagalla, the head man who first greeted Delumi on the verandah with his son and daughter-in-law, happened to be sitting smoking further along the verandah; he spoke to the child in her native tongue. She immediately walked over to Delumi and stood looking at her, eyes very wide.

"What is your name dear?" Delumi asked.

"Jacinta!" The little girl whispered, tucking her chin into her chest.

"Oh! What a pretty name, I think that must be a wild flower of the desert, don't you?" Delumi mentioned her own name, then queried. "You don't see many white ladies, do you?"

Jacinta nodded, and then said.

"Miss Manning my teacher is white and so is Missus Rosie, the doctor; she is white too!"

"Oh, I see. And what do you find different with me?"

Delumi looked whimsically at Jacinta, who put tongue in cheek for a second, then blurted.

"Why have you got funny eyes – are they sick?" Taken aback, Delumi faltered.

"Why, no Jacinta, my eyes are not sick. What makes you say that? Oh! I know. It is just their natural colour Dear; there is nothing wrong with my eyes. You see, there are lots and lots of white people with very pale blue eyes like mine! Do you want a closer look?" Delumi leaned forwards so that the child could see better.

"Mmphf!" Jacinta moved nearer and hugged Delumi's knee. Delumi stroked the black hair and they chatted away merrily until Jacinta was called by her mother. They waved goodbye to each other. Soon Delumi was taken to her sleeping quarters and quiet descended over the household.

A hive of activity about the station and it's stockyards had Delumi awakened just after sun-up. Horses milling and men jabbering to the tinkle of bits and stirrup irons mixed with the barking of dogs, heralded the start of a new day. For half an hour, bedlam reigned all about; then as men and horses rode off into the distance escorted by the dogs, quiet became the norm. Delumi freshened herself up and was then led into the kitchen, where the womenfolk partook of a morning meal; more enjoyable after the men had been fed and gone to work. It was well into the mid-morning before the drone of her Cessna could be heard in the distance. Alone, Delumi would not have known it was coming but the excited jabbering of the children outside pointing to the east, had the ladies of the household spread along the verandah to witness the approaching aircraft. The station boasted a makeshift runway downwind from the dwellings, but it was rarely used; hence the excitement of the youngsters. As Wally was left behind to guard the old men, women and children, it fell to him to take Delumi in the utility to meet the visiting aeroplane. Those children who could not fit into the back, charged after them on foot, discreetly followed by some of the young ladies. Justin Jurgens was Delumi's pilot and close friend. It was he who alighted first and hugged her when she arrived. Also aboard the Cessna, was

Delumi's secretary, Maureen Darnell; she too, hugged Delumi. The visitors were introduced to Wally who was immediately invited to help unload the Cessna. The largest baggage was the medium sized motorcycle, somehow wedged into the two rear seats compartment; made possible only because of the front wheel having been removed. With Wally's help, eventually it was properly assembled, fuelled and ready to go. With a huge grin on his face, Wally lovingly eyed the sparkling new machine, almost jealously.

"Ay Missus!" He eagerly asked. "You not riding this one back to the mine are you?"

"No Wally, I will go back in my Cessna!"

Both Delumi and Justin seemed to be enjoying a huge joke. Wally puzzled.

"Whyfor you bring this feller then?" Delumi placed her hand upon Wally's shoulder.

"Wally Dear. You saved my life out there in the desert and I heard you broke your own motorbike, so this is my way of saying, thank you. This motorcycle is for you so you can get back home. It is a small payment for saving my life Wally – thank you once again!"

Delumi kissed his cheek.

"Crikey!" Wally was almost speechless. He sat astride the machine apparently suddenly shy and overcome. He gave a great toothy grin to Delumi.

"Wallaballagalla sure is one lucky feller – ay?"

"Well don't just sit there Wally – go for a ride!" Justin urged.

Wally needed no second urging. With glowing face and radiant grin, he set the motor purring and disappeared with a billowing trail of choking dust. The three white folk placed two suitcases into in the back of the utility, called upon the children to climb aboard, and then Justin drove back to the main house. One of the suitcases contained clothing and a vanity satchel for Delumi, the other was full of gifts for the immediate household; including sweets and minor toys for the children. That the young business executive thought to organise and managed to have accomplished this feat, having barely scraped to safety from a terrible demise in the cruel Australian outback; proved her ability and expertise in that capacity to which she aspired and performed so well. The white visitors remained at the station only long enough for refreshments, presenting the gifts and to await Wally's return, before taking their leave with a promise to return soon for a conference with Djinda, the head man, and the tribal elders. There was quite a huge crowd of people who came to wave farewell to them, as the party taxied off in the Cessna. Delumi felt extremely grateful that she was alive and well and able to leave. But for the arrival of Wally she may never have been making this flight. Her thoughts reverted to that evening on the verandah and the cute little face of Jacinta – yes – Delumi would return; and very soon, as she had taken a liking to these wonderful carefree and most courteous people. In transit, the aircraft passed the main group of men out in the light scrub, where they were rounding up the cattle prior to tagging the stock they were to prepare for market. When those aboard espied the huge bulk of Djinda, more noticeable because of his flowing white beard. Delumi had Justin dip the wings of the Cessna in the traditional wave of recognition and farewell or welcome. Many hats were raised in response. In less than one hour the Cessna was landing at the mine airstrip and the two ladies were whisked away in the chauffer-driven limousine, which was awaiting them. Justin went about the business of supervising the maintenance and preparation of their aircraft, so as it would be in readiness and available to the whims and needs of his managing director, when she had attended her business dealings with the mine management. This, Justin was assured, would not take long; nor did it. Within two more hours, the three were dining in the members bar of the Mine Company Hotel, a most modern building built for the mining fraternity on the outskirts of the nearby township, which was just as isolated in the outback of Australia, as the mine to which it belonged.

"Beats bush tucker, wouldn't you say, Del?" Justin stated.

"Now do not go denigrating bush tucker Justin!" Delumi cautioned. "It was a life-saver for me, but I must acknowledge that first real meal with the Ballagalla's, although quite palatable and enjoyable; is not the same as these commercial preparations with their delicacies and spices!"

"Oh! Me for 'Liszt Austrian Restaurant' in Melbourne or even the famous 'Escargot de Paris' at Bondi – there is manna from heaven!" Maureen crooned wistfully.

"Dear me Maureen, you sound like a spoiled brat!" Delumi expostulated. "And as for bush tucker – I tell you – Wally's burned lizard was a culinary treat to a famished damsel in distress.

Thank the powers that be for Wallaballagalla and the Ballagalla people. I swear they will live forever in my dreams – bless them!"

Once again back into the swing of her business life-style, Delumi began to be the vibrant young executive that her peers and fellow workers knew. Hers was the bustling time-measured madness of the modern society in which she lived and flourished. Hectic schedules and boardroom conferences were her lot for the following two weeks or so, but ever in her mind was the peaceful life-style of the Ballagalla's with whom she had spent a wasted week. But was it truly wasted? Delumi felt that fate had ordained she be thrust upon them, albeit in such drastic and violent circumstances. She felt that there must be a deeper and more profound reason for that frightening experience; so foreign to such a sheltered white executive! The thought preyed upon her young and agile mind to such an extent, that it was with a little less trepidation and a very positive and even eager outlook, that she finalised plans to continue with the work pursuant to the contract that she and Thurston Klotz initiated almost one month earlier. New contracts were drawn up using the drafts of those destroyed with the explosion and burning of the limousine; almost identical copies as laid down by her employer, Thurston. In his name and for his widow, Delumi felt it her duty to honour and complete that undertaking, so that the death of her good friend and employer, was not in vain! With the contract details finalised and Maureen at hand, Justin was once more required to take them back to the remote gold mine; Delumi at once eager and with great confidence that a suitable settlement could be arrived at with the mining company. When Klotz Holdings and Investments Limited acquired the proof that worthwhile ore deposits were in the land they researched, long leases were contracted to them by the Government. Now was the ticklish time of making a solid and set case for the mining company to be interested enough, to sub-lease this land for mining; affording the K.H.I.L., a handsome profit. Delumi's only concern now was to find out what native title if any, was valid. The Government had no known records of existing native requirements for the land. It was Delumi's fervent hope that there would be none. She felt it may be a forlorn hope though! The Gold Mine was a privately owned concern with its greater majority of shares restricted to family members. The minor forty nine percent being retained by public stockholders, most of who were in the large city of Kalgoorlie, hundreds of kilometres further west. Here was situated the head office of the mining company. For expediency, arrangements were made for a meeting of the mine management and the K.H.I.L. contingent, to be held in the executive suite of the Mine Company Hotel. With the initial details of the area involved, the assayer's report and the cubic capacity of the land in question discussed; the next move was to be a visual aerial inspection. As Delumi's Cessna seated but six, the larger Lear Jet of the mine executives was employed. Justin remained behind with the Cessna to clean and coddle the machine. The inspection and surveying of the new territory to be mined completed, another discussion was held over lunch. The mining company confirmed that indeed, the vast plains and lower hills of the intended contract were known to be of significant spiritual value of the local tribe – believed to be the Ballagalla's! Until a clearance with the Ballagalla's was obtained, all dealings would have to be put on 'hold'! Although a little in doubt, Delumi fancied that a suitable arrangement could be contrived with the Ballagalla's. To this end, Delumi rang Djindagarra.

Chapter Three

THE CORROBOREE

Delumi Vido, Maureen Darnell and Justin Jurgens, were welcomed by Djindagarra and his immediate family, when they arrived at the cattle station. Around the table, they sat in conference sipping at tea and home-made honey spiced damper. Also upon the table was one of the six large fruit cakes which the visitors brought with them for the families to share; presuming they would be a treat for the children who may not often sample such fare, out this far from the busy cities. Upon asking about the health and whereabouts of Wallaballagalla, Djinda informed Delumi that his intended month or so visit was cut short, due to his becoming the proud owner of a new motorbike.

"Nah! That Wally, he don't want to waste his time 'round here just looking at his bike. After two weeks he couldn't hang about no more an' he just took off – reckon he wanted to get back home and show off to his family – ay?" Djinda smiled hugely as he stroked his white beard.

"Oh I am so glad he was pleased with my gift. He really deserved it!" Delumi stated, and then became serious.

"I suppose you realised that this is not just a social visit, seeing as I brought my secretary with me to take notes?" Delumi raised her eyebrows in query as she spoke. "When the elders heard you wanted to visit and we knew you'd been to the mine, they got their heads together – it has to do with our homeland – don't it?" Djinda asked. Delumi nodded, as Maureen noted the conversation in her notebook in short-hand; then stated. "Klotz Holdings and Investments Limited has leased the land north of the mine and to the east as far as the Ballagalla western boundary. We have it leased for a fifty year period. However, we need to know how mining the land would affect the Ballagalla people and what, if any, are the spiritual ties your people have with that land!" Delumi paused for a little. "You see Djinda; we will not put business before your tribal beliefs and needs. Klotz Holdings feel they owe the Ballagalla's much respect and friendship. We will be entirely guided by the elders of the tribe, so we have come to ask them for a ruling and their blessing for us to sub-lease the land to the mine. Remember, there will be a percentage of profits to the Ballagalla's and many of them will find long employment at the new workings!" Delumi rested her case, waiting expectantly.

In their own dialect, those elders present, who included the head man of the tribe, Balla Ballagalla, discussed the matter raised; at some length, they constantly asked Djindagarra questions. Patiently, Delumi and her staff waited. Maureen, dismayed that she could not take notes as the tribal tongue was too quick even for her fast shorthand. Even so, that shorthand would have had to be interpreted! Eventually the tribal elders became silent, leaving Djinda to express their reply.

"Delumi! The elders are very pleased the way you come to ask. You know – most white ones just take an' don't worry about our feelings or dreamings!" Djinda smiled warmly. "But!" He continued. "This is a matter for all of the Ballagalla's to discuss, not just the family. We can't decide alone – you understand?" Delumi nodded.

"How long will it take to discuss it properly?" She politely asked. Balla Ballagalla spoke up.

"Maybe two – three weeks, must make Corroboree!"

Delumi was surprised.

"Oh! Really; are white people allowed to come to the corroboree?" Djinda answered. "Yes, this one is okay, it is not a spiritual meeting or an initiation; it's just a gathering of the elders to make a ruling. They will discuss the wishes of the spirits of our ancestors. You sure to be welcome but must not interfere with dreamtime talk!"

Balla Ballagalla spoke in their tribal tongue to his son, Djinda, and then pointed with his pipe at Delumi; she looked expectantly to Djinda for an interpretation.

"Dad said I should explain to you that at one time the corroboree was only men's business. It was forbidden to the women and all outsiders, but nowadays, what with us blokes doing more white fellow things; like ranching and farming and driving earthmoving equipment, not to mention the trade in aboriginal artefacts – you know – boomerangs, paintings and that sort of stuff; also the tourism trade. Well, naturally we had to show off our dancing – mind you – it's only tourist corroboree you people see, just for little things!"

"Then you still hold old-fashioned corroborees?" Delumi asked, wide-eyed.

"Too right!" Djinda confirmed, eyes lighting up. "Just like you people do in the cities. We have our high courts too, for serious stuff. As I said before – initiations, family disputes, land rights between tribes – all that sort of business!" Delumi was really interested now.

"What about pointing the bone?" Balla Ballagalla spoke sharply to his son. Djinda frowned.

"Better go a bit easy Delumi, you might upset the oldies. They don't like too much of our tribal business known to outsiders; better if we changed the subject I reckon!"

Delumi blushed. A thing she rarely did.

"Oh, Djinda, please forgive me!" She turned to Balla Ballagalla. "I'm sorry!"

He nodded. That was the end of it.

After stating her business and having been assured she would be contacted by Djinda in good time to witness the corroboree, when all the elders involved were gathered, Delumi and her staff made their departure. She felt her meeting was well received by the tribe and her chances of a favourable settlement enhanced by the way her honest and open approach was appreciated. The few weeks of waiting for word from Djinda, gave Delumi time to ponder upon another bright idea with which she had been toying. Presuming that the outcome of this latest enterprise would be favourable to the Klotz Holdings and Investments Limited, Delumi deemed it wise to offer a bonus which would not only benefit the Ballagalla's, but would also leave her with a sense of gratification and fulfilment for their welfare, of which she could be proud. She would make the necessary enquiries regarding the viability and costing of this undertaking; before suggesting it to the tribal elders. After all settlements were satisfactorily accomplished Delumi deemed, would be the appropriate time to offer her suggestion.

It was just over two weeks before Delumi and her 'entourage' were again at the cattle station, all agog with high expectations and with just a little trepidation, at the thought of being the only three white folk amongst the black community at a real tribal corroboree. That the dancers would all be painted in ochre and bedecked with feathered plumes, Delumi did not doubt. In her mind she could picture dozens of heaving black bodies wielding boomerangs and spears, as they stomped around a camp-fire. Mental pictures of a movie she had seen of the American Indians doing a war-dance, was prevalent in her thoughts; perhaps the Aborigines of Australia did something of a similar nature? Delumi, Maureen and Justin were all agreed that they would be secreted away to some remote bush setting to a spiritual site for this ceremony. They were somewhat deflated to find that the site of the ceremony was to be within easy walking distance of the homestead and just far enough away from the stables, so that the horses would not be adversely affected. Only one or two aborigines could be seen about with any sort of war paint at all adorning them. Indeed, most of the elders whom they knew were dressed in their everyday working clothes. There was even a barbeque warming up with plastic containers choc-a-bloc full of steak slabs.

"Gosh! I am a little disappointed!" Justin quietly said.

"Yes." Maureen offered. "It appears as if we are just having a back yard barbeque!"

Delumi cautioned.

"Don't show any disappointment, let us just wait and see!"

Djinda and his large family, including his mother and father, emerged from the house. Wally had motored over on his new machine especially for the occasion and he had been the person who was attending the three white guests. He had left them momentarily to find out how long it would be before the guests could take their places, for the ceremony. Wally spoke to them as he arrived back.

"We just walk over slow-like. Boss-man and the elders sit first, then we sit with them – ay?" The guests discreetly followed the chiefs. Behind them, came those members of the tribes who would take no active part in the corroboree. The children were to be amongst these except those older boys who would soon arrive at warrior status; they would be allowed to dance the corroboree. This was to be a learning experience for them all. The elders walked well past the barbeque and it was only then that the visitors noticed the huge unlit bonfire, around which the leading party gathered. Balla Ballagalla began an intonation in his native dialect. He droned on for five minutes before the others in the circle joined in, then a flint was struck and the bonfire lit. More intonations and then, in turn, the elders took their places squatting upon the ground facing the radiant flames; flickering shadows danced upon the stern ebon features. The guests were seated next to Djinda's eldest son, Johnny, who was the outsider of the main group. As the rest of the aborigines took their respective places, the chanting continued, others joining in as they became seated. It was then apparent why the guests were seated beside Johnny. Being the eldest son of the tribal elder and having the best command of English, it fell to him to interpret the proceedings as it was to be in tribal language in it's entirety! Johnny did not whisper, for the chanting was quite loud and the guests were hard put to hear him anyhow. "Balla is blessing the ceremony and asking the spirits of our ancestors to give wisdom to the elders for this important decision!" Johnny enlightened. "They'll yabber on for another half hour like this, then when Balla begins to tell the children the story of how light same upon our land, most of the fighting men will begin to don the ceremonial trappings!" Not being able to understand the words, the ceremony was beginning to bore the white visitors. Of a sudden, Balla rose and waved to all about. As the warriors began their make-up, the children gathered about Balla who was by now, alone; the other elders preparing for the dance. Johnny stayed by the guest's side and began interpreting Balla's story of the light. This is how it was translated:-

'In the beginning the earth was in darkness. Amongst the black people of the land at that time, lived a man whose name was Dityi. In his tribe he took a very beautiful woman named Mitjen as his wife. At first they were very happy and they loved each other very much. There were no white men at that time and the black people thought that where they lived and hunted to the far hills was the whole world. But a stranger came to camp. A tall man named Bunjil. He told stories of the far away forests and the wonderful things to be found there, Mitjen was most interested. Eventually Bunjil took Mitjen away with him, back to the land of the forests. Her tribe was very angry and offended. They fell into a great rage and painted themselves with clay, took up arms and were led by Dityi, but they could not find where Bunjil and Mitjen had gone. All returned their own land and families. Dityi struggled on alone seeking his lost love. Mitjen found that Bunjil did not love her and only wanted her to cook for him and help him hunt for food. Mitjen missed her husband who looked after her and loved her and she wanted to go back. Bunjil would not let her, so he beat her and kicked her as she slept. One time Mitjen did not wake. Bunjil had killed her. Then a great storm came upon the land and sucked Bunjil up into the darkness of the sky. Now if you look closely, you may see him; wandering across the void, a lonely star, finding no rest anywhere and without a mate or a home. The other stars go away from him if they cross his path. Mitjen also went gently up into the sky, taken by that storm. There she saw Ditji who lit up the sky, for he had turned into the sun and was giving light to the earth. Always the black people say he is seeking Mitjen. His wurley is in Nganat, just over the edge of the earth and the bright sunset colours are caused by the dead going in and out of Nganat, as Ditji looks amongst them for his lost love. Mitjen, Mitjen! He calls. It is then that we hear the thunder, but Mitjen never answers. She has been made the moon and always she mourns, far away and alone for her Ditji. When she hears his noise and the rumble of his trampling feet, she hides away for she is ashamed. She only comes out of her hiding place when he is asleep. Sometimes Mitjen heaves a great sigh and that is the wind and her tears are the rain. That is how light come upon the earth!"

As Balla Ballagalla, the head man, finished the telling of the tribal legend of daylight with a large sweep of his outstretched arm; there was silence. The children sat in awe, their eyes wide with wonder and more than one mouth agape. Balla ordered the children to clear the area around the fire and return to their family places; this they did. Two women began beating a hollow log with sticks to a steady rhythm. Six warriors entered the firelight, stamping their feet to the beat, each clacking a pair of boomerangs together in tune. They were mainly daubed with streaks of white and many dots upon what bare skin seemed available. The men wore 'g' strings and a bunch of feathers adorned their nether regions in the manner of birds' tails; a few feathers also stuck in their hair. As these six danced and stomped before the head man and in front of the fire, more similarly outfitted warriors joined in the festivities. With a full compliment of approximately fifty dancers, including fifteen or so older boys and youths, the chanting began again and as it got louder, turned into song. Occasionally a high-pitched shout echoed from the frenzied, gyrating mass of dark bodies, with white flashes of reflection from the flames off the white markings which flickered, exaggerating the movements. About one dozen of the dancers were handed long hunting spears as they cavorted about, now all of the feet stomping dancers moved in one direction around the fire. As those with spears passed the whites, they advanced menacingly and pretended to be spearing guests. Johnny cautioned the three to stay calm and still as they would not be harmed. It was only a part of the ritual, an important part in which all evil spirits were being chased away so that the elders could make the good and clean decision to honour the spirits of their ancestors; without any bad or evil influences about. It was a timely warning as Maureen all but screamed in fright at the first onslaught. The dancing lasted a good hour, but the guests did not notice it pass; they were as spellbound by the dancers as the children were with Balla's story. Justin studied the make up of the dancers. He asked Johnny a question.

““What feathers do they use – is it Emu feathers?”

“Yes! Emu feathers, some very old and steeped in family tradition. They get passed down through the generations – same as those tufts of grass on the ankles, wrists and elbows. Some are what you know as 'Pampas Grass', other kinds they sometimes hang from their 'g' strings are religious tufts from circumcision initiation rituals!” The guests were impressed.

The fire began to die and no more fuel was applied to keep it burning. The younger children had been taken by their mothers in dribs and drabs according to their ages and the fact that they could no longer keep their eyes open. Only the more dedicated fighting men continued the dance. By this time the barbecue food was prepared and most of the children and some of the ladies had eaten. The senior men sat with the elders as the flames began their last hurrah, for now was the hour of deep consultation; the spirits having been appeased and the main topic on the agenda well into consideration! Johnny led the three white people to the barbeque area and bade them help themselves, saying.

“The old fellers make real big talk now. We all just wait, when Balla Ballagalla and the other elders have finished eating and after their big talk – or maybe while they are eating – they will ask for you to join them at the corroboree fire. That is when you get an answer one way or the other!”

Delumi led the way by picking up a paper plate, heaping food upon it and standing aside whilst the others did likewise; then they joined her. The three conversed quietly amongst themselves as they partook of their food. Johnny left them there and went to await the elders call for him.

Chapter Four

A CHANGE OF FORMAT

Wallaballagalla was one of those warriors still dancing, his heaving body as agile as if he had barely begun! As they ate, Delumi, Maureen and Justin, watched the few remaining dancers from afar, occasionally glancing in the direction of the elders; deep in conversation. The beating of the hollow log ceased; the clacking of the boomerangs was no more. With final shouts, all those about the dying fire departed; the dancers heading for food and drinks whilst the elders summoned Johnny to bring the guests over to them. A decision had been made! Balla Ballagalla bade the guests sit upon the ground with the elders, forming a large circle so as each person could see eye-to-eye with all others, at that meeting. He spoke in his native dialect grandiosely, then in English for the benefit of the guests.

"The big-feller elder's bin make corroboree and talk with our ancestors and the spirits of the land and the skies above!" He swept both arms about indicating those elders and the land and the sky. "We bin talk with peera (the moon) and the whisper of our land. Ballagalla's see honest faces of friends and ask white ones to sign paper for Djindagarra, an' be true one-time and for all-time, to Ballagalla's!" Balla looked keenly and deeply into Delumi's face.

Delumi's serious face and a slight nod, was accompanied by a solemn promise.

"I will see that the Ballagalla Nation and Tribes will be properly looked after and that they will be legally covered in accordance with our earlier proposition. I give the elders my solemn promise!" Johnny interpreted her statement. It was well received as the elders all nodded.

"Ballagalla's lending our ancestral land to white people, from Ballagalla Station boundary to Western Hills and North in land of Bunjil!"

Balla and the elders had spoken; it was to be so! As the elders began rising to have their belated meal, Delumi called.

"Wait!" Surprised, all turned to her. "Please sit. I wish to say something. It will be very short!"

Balla nodded and all regained their places. They looked expectantly to Delumi, wondering.

"Because we are going to work together for the benefit of us all, I want to offer something to the Ballagalla's in friendship and on behalf of my company – K.H.I.Limited!"

She turned to Johnny.

"Would you please interpret so the elders understand fully what I am proposing?"

Delumi went straight into her proposal.

"On behalf of my company, I want to organise for the younger Ballagalla's, a twice-yearly holiday package, which will take the children on holiday camps and guided tours of the big cities, the mine and other places of learning. Places such as Uluru (Ayers Rock), Kata Tjuta (Mt. Olga), the Museum etcetera! All paid for by K.H.I.L. and properly supervised by your own people – you know – Djindagarra (if he wants to and is able), Wallagallaballa, Johnny and some of the children's mothers! Please, would you let me do this?"

The elders conducted a short conference, and then spoke to Johnny. Leaving him to tell Delumi of their decision; they left and began their belated supper. Johnny had a huge grin. "Hey! That was a master-stroke. The elders are very impressed and see a good benefit in this whole enterprise. They reckon the Ballagalla's are in an all-win situation. With the kids and the holidays – they said yes and thanks – but I have to supervise and be responsible for all dealings with you Delumi; my dad will be too busy running the cattle station. But yes. It is all go-ahead!"

While the elders ate and drank, many women were dragging more wood from a storage shed, to the glowing embers. The fire was being re-kindled! Justin caught young Wally by the elbow as he passed with a chop in one hand and a drink in the other.

"Hey Wally!" He urgently asked. "What's going on – why is the fire being built up?"

"Celebration! Elders say spirits of our ancestors sing with us tonight. Peera, the moon, hides no more and we dance with Peera until her face is covered; then we know it is time to rest. Ballagalla's celebrate new work coming and much good over our land and we are happy – so we celebrate at corroboree!"

He wandered over to the corroboree fire and after having partaken of the refreshments, began to dance with his fellow warriors. Meanwhile, Delumi and Maureen were conversing with Djinda, who was in his ceremonial trappings. He looked a magnificent specimen of manhood as he chatted casually with these females of another race. Djindagarra was a striking example of the warrior who is born to lead his peoples, the flowing white beard enhancing the well-muscled frame, although belying the great physical strength evident now by the scant attire of the fighting man.

"You are at liberty to retire if you so desire!" He told the young ladies. "The sky is quite clear and we may dance all night!"" Delumi thanked him and then, with Maureen; sought Justin.

"What would you two like to do?" She asked of them. "Shall we stay here overnight? As there are three of us and the station has many other guests here, perhaps we should unpack the tents and camp out!"

"Oh, no! I don't fancy that with all these aborigines from other places gathered here – shouldn't we fly back to the comfort of the Mine Hotel?" Maureen worried.

"Yes, I think I would prefer that – it is only an hour or so away and the night is still young – we can return tomorrow for the paper signings!" Justin suggested.

"You have seen enough corroboree?" Delumi queried. Her staff nodded in unison.

As Djinda, Johnny and Wally were all dancing and stomping by the corroboree fire, the three white guests sought Balla Ballagalla, the head man, as he sat with the other elders witnessing the celebrations. He was chanting, but ceased as the trio neared him. He rose to greet them, a huge smile upon his face. Delumi thanked him for inviting them to the corroboree and asked his permission to leave and fly back to the hotel. They would return the next day in the afternoon, if that was agreeable to him. The guests left with the blessing of the elders. Bright and early the next morning, Delumi rang Johnny and arrangements were made with the Ballagalla's legal representatives, to have the necessary documents amended and signed. Within one week, the business between the K.H.I.L. and the mining company was satisfactorily accomplished to the mutual benefit and satisfaction of all partners involved. Delumi offered Maureen a holiday package for three weeks but retained Justin to accompany her as chauffeur and escort; deeming that a working holiday was in store for both of them. Delumi's intent was to have a restful break from business herself, whilst tying some loose ends with the arrangements she had instigated at tourist destinations; with the Ballagalla children in mind. They set off for Ayers Rock, in Central Australia; flying there in the Cessna. It was not the ideal time of year to be heading for Central Australia. Summer was well and truly evident. Clear skies with balmy days of sand-flies and night-time buzzing mosquitoes, did not make for a very comfortable holiday. Once in the Cessna, air control was just a small matter of buttons and levers; but down upon the ground one had an urgent need to quit the aircraft and hasten to the air-conditioned comfort of a hotel or guest house, with the utmost speed. Blistering heat outside and annoying pesky little winged horrors, determined to avoid the great Australian Salute and suck at one's perspiring brow or neck, made for an unbearable pastime out-of-doors. When the two young travellers landed in their aircraft at the large hotel-motel complex, situated just ten or so kilometres from that vast monolith of the Australian Desert, named Ayers

Rock by white explorers; then by legislation regaining it's original name as known by the indigenous peoples – Uluru - they were thankful that the air-conditioned chauffeur-driven limousine was all ready and waiting for them! Delumi and Justin motored to the comforts of the luxurious apartments and a refreshing cool drink. They looked forwards to a sumptuous meal in elegant and refined surroundings, with perhaps a nice quiet evening of dancing!

It was during lunch when they partook of a seafood salad, that Delumi noticed a clean-cut man of neat appearance discreetly glancing her way every now and again. She noted that he was quite solid in build and appeared to be the athletic type. Their eyes met and he smiled at Delumi. She politely acknowledged his attention with a coy smile of her own; then engaged

Justin in trivial conversation. Delumi sensed the other man was still discreetly looking her way on occasions. Presently, a steward appeared bearing a tray upon which was a bottle of light wine. "Pardon Madam, compliments of Mister Carrens. He requests that you and your husband should honour him with your presence at your convenience, after you have lunched!" He waited expectantly. Delumi asked. 'Who is Mister Carrens?" Although she realised that it could be none other than the man who was watching; he was not known to her.

"Oh dear!" The steward answered. "I thought everyone knew Mister Carrens. He is the movie producer doing the Documentary on Uluru! Payne Carrens is a quite important personality of late around here. He and his crew have brought this area alive over the past few weeks!"

"I see!" Delumi pondered the situation. "Do you know why he is dining alone? Where are his crew and advisors?" The steward nodded knowingly.

"They were dining with him but most retired to the pool-side to digest their meal and relax before the next filming takes place. Mister Carrens declined to go with them when he noticed you people enter. He may see you as a star for his filming, you know!" Delumi glanced in the direction of Payne Carrens. He smiled again, a query on his features.

"Ask Mister Carrens to give us a half hour, we shall see him in the lounge – oh! Thank Mister Carrens for the wine but we have had enough!" The steward went upon his errand.

As Justin held the door of the lounge ajar for Delumi, they saw Payne Carrens arise and approach them with hand outstretched.

"Thank you for giving me your time and please excuse me for interrupting your lunch!" Introductions were made.

"Oh!" Payne apologised. "I stupidly assumed you were husband and wife – do forgive me!" Delumi waved aside the faux-pas as Justin blushed; she discreetly pretended not to notice her pilot's embarrassment at the situation suddenly thrust upon him.

"Let us sit Mister Carrens – what is it you wish to discuss with us – I understand you are filming in this area. I assume that is the topic of this meeting?" Delumi raised her eyebrows expectantly.

"My word, you are perceptive and well-informed, yet you have barely arrived here!" Payne stated, with a bland smile.

"The waiter!" Delumi explained.

"Ah! Of course!" Payne Carren's brow furrowed as he showed slight embarrassment as he outlined his dilemma. "I am making a documentary film of Ayers Rock – Uluru – and I have twin problems which are bugging the project at the moment!"

He paused and took a deep breath as he studied the reactions of his listeners. Payne continued.

"I dearly hope and pray that you people can alter your schedule and stay here for a week or perhaps more, to help me and my crew out of a very sticky situation!"

He earnestly scanned their faces for the slightest hint of them assenting to this possibility.

Delumi sat with passive features, patiently awaiting Payne Carrens' proposal. He let a huge smile envelope his quite handsome face as he chose his words carefully. No doubt sensing that these people, upon whom he was reliant, were self-sufficient and did not need him or his propositions. Indeed, it was he who had to be quite tactful and a little sub-servient, to attain his ends. This smart young pair would not easily be led, as were the majority of the cast with whom he dealt and the many aspiring young would-be stars and hangers-on; usually associated with the film industry.

"Miss Vido - !"

"Delumi!" She cut in.

"Thank you – Delumi -, you are the essence of a director's dream. When first I witnessed you exit your Cessna and saw the poise and grace of your deportment, the commanding and yet genteel manner in which you conduct yourself and the very evident fact that you are a most intelligent person - I dared hope that you might be willing to come to my assistance. In filming, we had a mis-hap! My presenter – Naomi Progue – had a fall and not only broke her ankle but suffered a nasty gash to the cheek. Make-up could do little about that. Oh sure, they covered the gash and stitches but the large swelling of poor Naomi's cheek could not be hidden!" Payne took a deep breath. "I need a smart, pretty presenter, Delumi. Would you help me, please?" He implored.

Delumi pouted, deliberating the offer. It was more or less what she had expected to hear from Payne.

"You mentioned twin problems?" Delumi raised an eyebrow again.

Payne half expected Delumi to be flattered by his proposal and her quiet response took him unawares.

"Oh! Er, yes! Your Cessna – our camera plane is grounded due to mechanical failure. We have to wait for parts to arrive. You see, the script calls for an aerial view of a Cessna flying around Ayers Rock and we need another aircraft from which to film it!"

Delumi nodded absently, and then asked.

"As we approached the landing strip I noticed many other aircraft about were they not suitable?" Payne sighed as he shook his head.

"Believe me, I have asked, quite desperately I might add. I have staff and equipment remaining idle and costing huge amounts so I certainly have been a pushy person of late; unfortunately all other aircraft are on tight schedules and definitely not available. Not at such short notice anyway – I really am desperate – can you; will you help me?"

The strain upon his face was noticeably evident.

Delumi looked at her pilot. Justin shrugged, and then gave a slight nod.

"Presuming we are available Payne, would you spell out in detail what is expected of us, what input you require and give us a firm length of undertaking? We do have other commitments lined up!"

She equipped herself with the appointment book from her handbag and perused it minutely as she listened to the excited producer. Feelings of intrigue and wonder caressed her subconscious as Delumi took in the details being outlined to her, of this challenging new experience unfolding before her. Payne Carrens was a glib orator, yet Delumi detected an underlying sincerity in his eloquence and her own curiosity was piqued to the extent that she began to look forwards to her impromptu screen test, arranged for one hour after the evening meal that day. Urgency had Payne excuse himself to quickly organize the first testing. Delumi rang her legal advisors in regard to contract guidance. Justin would not be required to do more than fly the Cessna to the whims of the film director. Although he would have a film crew as passengers and his mission would no doubt involve circling the very large monolith named - Uluru – by the Indigenous Australians; there was no doubt it would be just another day – or week – at the office for him.

"Much of a holiday we are likely to get Justin, does it bother you?"

Delumi asked, as the two relaxed in the lounge to discuss this latest escapade which the vibrant young executive seemed prone to succumb to at each and every turning. Her life had appeared to be that way of late, just get over one thing and something entirely different, would crop up. Ah well, it does add spice to life.

"Not at all Del', I think I may have a liking for a change of format – you did promise me a bus-man's holiday after all and that is just what I am getting, by all points so far!"

Justin had a boyish grin on his bright-eyed face. Delumi could see he was not at all put out by this unexpected change of plans;

in fact he could even be accused of viewing this episode as a new challenge and was all agog with excited eagerness to begin! They chatted idly about the day's events and what a week's delay may do to their other plans. There were no concrete arrangements made which would be interrupted by their sojourn into the film industry, so they relaxed whilst they could.

Chapter Five

THE MOVIE STAR

Passing her screen test with flying colours, Delumi was very pleased when Payne announced that one screen test was sufficient. Due to her position of command and authority within the Klotz Holdings and Investments Limited Empire, her natural leadership came to the fore in the screen test. To her, it was just another board meeting with the script akin to one of her rehearsed papers that was to be tabled. Used to being the focus of attention and a focal point herself, the cameras were no new experience to Delumi; it was as if she were born to the part of a movie presenter. Payne could barely believe his good fortune in snaring such a valuable stand-in! The script itself was an eye-opener for Delumi. It held all of the information which she had come to gather in her quest for the education of the Ballagalla children. She decided to make it a part of her contract, that the used scripts become available to her for translation into the Ballagalla dialect. Payne was more than pleased to arrange this, in fact offering a free copy of the finished product when filming ceased; not to be used until one month after the travelogue had premiered. Delumi knew that her film debut was actually a blessing in disguise. At sun-up the following morning, Delumi was hurrying to her first appointment with the director to overlay prior work already canned by the unfortunate Naomi, when she almost collided with the star at a doorway. Naomi was on crutches and her swollen face was quite evident, although the bruising was well painted over.

"Oh! I am sorry – you must be Naomi!" Delumi addressed her.

"Yes. Have we met before? I don't remember you!" Naomi frowned.

Delumi introduced herself.

"I am your stand-in; Payne twisted my arm!"

"Oh!" Naomi stiltedly responded.

"I am deeply sorry for your misfortune, Naomi. What horrid luck for you. I hear you have a nasty cut too – it is well hidden. Surgeons are so experienced these days dear, don't you fret. I am sure it will heal well and not be noticeable at all – you are beautiful you know; no wonder Payne was worried!" Delumi smiled sympathetically.

Naomi allowed a somewhat sickly smile to cross her features.

"You too, are beautiful – a most beautiful lady indeed – I feel my position will be lost if you can perform at all in front of the cameras!" Her voice faltered in whimsical dismay.

Delumi placed a hand on Naomi's arm.

"Oh Naomi, don't go into a panic dear. I am only a fill in. Once this job is over, I shall be off and away. I have much more important things planned than a film career. I promise you, when you are back on deck it is full steam ahead as usual for you. Truly, I am just a fill in for a week!"

Naomi brightened.

"Really, you think so?"

"I know so. I am no film person. It is not my style at all. I do not like being told what to do. I am more in tune giving the orders to others. I am a business person and this is just an escapade to relieve the boredom of everyday office-work. I should not be doing this film presenter business at all; it is just that Payne was in a predicament and I do tend to help a lame dog. Besides, Payne is very persuasive!"

Delumi's' bright radiant smile brought a like response from Naomi.

"You had better scoot then, Delumi. Kurt Stols hates to be kept waiting – break a leg!"

Naomi waved her stand-in away.

"Eh? 0h – thanks!" Delumi hurried off.

As the new presenter approached the director, she could well understand Naomi's warning. Kurt Stols – for it could only be he – was pacing agitatedly about his crew with moustache bristling the while he tugged angrily at his goatee. The man was quite slight in stature when compared to the athletic bulk of his producer; in fact Kurt may be described as very weedy. What he lacked in stature he more than made up for in temperament. "Where have you been, do you think we have nothing better to do that to sit about waiting for Prima Donna's?" His tone was quite sharp. He continued almost in the same breath.

"Do you know you lines, are you properly made up? Stand there in front of that dropping; move girl – move – lights – camera, now children just a dry run – all ready? Action!"

Delumi was internally fuming. She all but gave the director a piece of her mind and told him what he could do with his lines – her lines – but then, he was a director and Delumi had understood them to be very temperamental people. It probably was par for the course to be temperamental, if one was a director. Delumi swallowed her pride and gave her best delivery possible - maybe to prove a point.

"Marvellous, marvellous!" Kurt clapped his hands and pranced about. "Alright children – just like that – do it again. This is a take!" The cast and crew swung into action again. "No, no, no, no – tut, tut, tut! Cut, cut!" Kurt screamed from his chair. "Girl, what is your name?"

He glared at Delumi. She responded with her name.

"Delumi Dear, I can forgive you once. You must only look into the lens. Don't go glancing around like a tourist – do you understand?" Kurt smiled, stroked his goatee, and then called.

"From the top children – ready? Action!"

And so the day progressed. To her credit there were very few re-takes needed. Delumi did her part well. At the lunch break, Payne was awaiting Delumi. He escorted her to the dining room.

"Kurt is very pleased with you Delumi. He says you have a great career ahead of you; have you given any thought to that at all?" Her wide eyes attested her surprise at his statement.

"Goodness Payne! I thought the director would have blasted me. Do you know how many re-takes I caused?"

Delumi sat as Payne attended her chair; he then sat opposite her at the table. "Yes. There were five!" He grinned, his eyes alight with pride. "Naomi took eighteen on her first photo call and seven on one shot alone. You have done very well, very well indeed. You see, not all re-takes are the star's fault. Sometimes it is the cameraman, lighting, audio or perhaps a prop may move. A good trouper takes that all in her stride – and just ignore Kurt's nasty remarks – he probably does not realise that he makes them. That is just the way of directors – everything must be just so! Did you find the work tiring?" His look of concern was genuine.

The new star gave a wry smile.

"Surprisingly – no – I rather enjoyed the challenge. I don't think I would care for a career in the business though!" Delumi pouted as she casually asked. "Does the producer always escort his leading ladies to lunch?"

Payne had just a tinge of being caught out on his cheeks.

"Well, it is certainly not unheard of, Delumi. I did think it was due you, just to help you fit in mind, seeing as how you are saving the company heaps by being available, and remember; we need your pilot and aircraft. It is imperative that I look after you!"

"Very plausible, Payne would you order a salmon salad for me, please?"

The steward was hovering nearby and the diners chatted casually as they partook of their meal. Looking about the dining area, Delumi remarked.

"I wonder what has happened to Justin. It doesn't feel like a meal without him!"

"Fear not!" Payne enlightened her. "He may still be doing circles around the big rock. I know he was scheduled to do a mid-day aerial to capture the blistering heat-haze. There could be many takes from different angles to properly capture the best shimmering effect of the vapour waves!"

"Ah, the poor Dear, and here we are in air-conditioned comfort living a life of luxury; I do feel for him!"

"So I gathered, Delumi. Just how deeply do you feel for him? Am I too bold in asking? Are the two of you really close – I mean – I don't see an engagement ring?"

Delumi studied Payne's frowning features for a little while, digesting the implications of his query.

"Justin and I have been very close friends for three or four years now, and I rely on him quite heavily at times. We are both free spirits and relish our independence. As for the crux of your query – She smiled flirtatiously - you will just have to guess and suffer a little Payne; won't you?" Delumi was enjoying this titillating moment.

"Horrid little urchin!" Payne growled; good-naturedly.

The meal dispatched, they went about their own duties. Delumi still in wonder at Justin's absence; she fervently hoped that nothing was amiss. No! Justin was too prepared and too good a pilot for any mishap to occur. Yet Delumi worried. There would be unaccustomed up-draughts over the monolith and after all, a Cessna was not a very large aircraft. Delumi had much faith in Justin' ability and cleared the worry from her mind as she mulled over her next part of the script. Before the break for the evening meal, Kurt Stols called his crew together for a briefing.

"Now children, listen carefully!" He commanded, waving his arms dramatically. "The weather people have been so sweet and they promised me that a dry low-pressure system is approaching. So we have to jump ahead quite a few takes, to pages one seventy five to one eighty two of your scripts. This is scenes twenty nine and thirty. Soak up every line and position until you know it backwards. We have a one hour break, then it is tinker-bell time and we must fly by night to our locations. The script calls for a good cloud cover and we may only get a short time suitable for filming. Children, do try to make all the scenes one take only. Thank you Dears; now off you toddle and be by the aircraft on time."

Delumi was delighted as she approached her usual table at the tea break. There sat Justin, chatting with Payne. Both were evidently awaiting her.

"Oh, Justin I am so glad to see you – I – I had a premonition that something was amiss, when you failed to turn up for lunch!" Justin was the first to stand as she approached, but it was Payne who was quick to attend her chair. "Thank you!" She smiled her appreciation. As all became seated, Justin remarked.

"Strange you should mention that Del'!" Her raised eyebrow begged an explanation.

"Up draught!" Justin said. "A narrow fissure on the Eastern side has a very strong up-draught compared to the other fissures that are wider. As the sun sets and the land cools, the hot winds suck off the flat lands and they double in strength towards the cooler evening. We got clipped a beauty by one gust and nearly lost a camera overboard. Luckily the cameraman and the camera were in their restraining belts. It was a bit hairy for a while!"

"Yes! My camera crews are sensible chaps and they do the right thing. Follow procedure and abide by all safety factors. It is part of their contracts, I pay a little above the award rates and the saving through lack of mishaps is quite substantial. It is the only way to get things done correctly and have a happy crew; who improve production accordingly!"

Payne grinned very smugly, proud of his record, Payne poured a little wine from the flagon on the table, into each of the three glasses laid out.

"Please, raise your glasses. I wish to salute both of you for your very successful beginnings and also to thank you for coming to our rescue – cheers!"

They touched glasses and sipped a little of the wine. Justin raised his glass to Payne.

"This toast is for you, Payne. I am thoroughly enjoying this experience and I know Delumi is too – so cheers to you also – and thanks for talking us into this madhouse!" Delumi concurred. Payne spoke, more to change the subject than anything else.

"I hope this depression coming is just the cloud cover we need and nothing more. A flood of rain is the last thing we want, thunder bursts can come up real suddenly out here!"

"I imagine it would be quite muddy too!" Delumi added.

"Heaven forbid!" Payne prayed.

"Sticky clag is more like it. No – the bureau is middling sure that it will be cloud cover only; just a little bit of rain!"

During the meal, Payne had lapsed into silence as Justin and Delumi caught up with each other's new experiences.

"Are you brooding Payne? You are awfully quiet!" Delumi noted.

"Ugh? Oh, er – no, no! I was surmising just what the relationship was with you and these Balywhatsit aborigine people. You know, that you are making a special effort on behalf of their children and all. What is that all about, do you mind telling me?" Delumi became enthusiastic.

"Why no, not at all Payne, Ballagalla is the tribal name and as the Managing Director of K.H.I.Limited, I needed their co-operation in a deal we had going with a large Mining Company. As a bonus to help the deal but mainly in appreciation of a service one of them did for me, personally; I promised to put together a package of cultural holidays for the children of the community. This is one of the main destinations I had in mind for them; so I came here to tie up loose ends and confirm accommodation arrangements!" She held out her open palms, expressively. "That's all there is to it!"

"You are Managing Director of Klotz Holdings and Investments Limited?" Payne asked, incredulously.

"Oh! You know us!" Delumi queried. Payne appeared almost apoplectic.

"Of course!" He replied. "We solicited your company for additional funding for our Kimberly Promotion. I think it fell through. Well, I must say, Delumi; I am flabbergasted. Imagine me having the temerity to think you were a Socialite on holidays and solicit you the way I did!"

He shook his head in wonder. Delumi giggled prettily.

"Ah! It adds spice to life, doesn't it? Perhaps you had better not let the matter pass this table Payne. We do not need complications, it will not help either of us – are we agreed?"

Payne nodded.

"My word yes, surely. I say, I shall certainly have to watch my step now. I cannot afford to displease you; that would really throw our schedule out!"

"Oh dear, Payne; do not fret. We have a contract and I for one, always honour contracts – rest easy – we are enjoying this!" Delumi smiled reassuringly. Payne sighed.

"Thanks; heck, I got a fright!"

Justin was delighted that his immediate boss had made such a great impact on the Film Producer; it elevated his status accordingly.

"You know now that you have a responsible leading lady, Payne!" Justin embellished. "And not a flippant Prima Donna of whimsies!"

He eyed the big man closely, enjoying his discomfort. Payne's attentions to Delumi had not been lost on her pilot, who realised the man was a rival for his interest in the pretty young lady. Being a quite astute person, Delumi was very aware of the slight rift between her admirers and addressed their attentions to her most pressing issue. "Payne, I know this current script has a focal point of Uluru but is Mount Olga or the Olga's a part of this travelogue?" Payne was all in favour of another line of conversation and jumped at the chance to air a little of his knowledge.

"No, we are making a thorough in-depth coverage of Uluru, and also of the Anangu – the aborigine custodians of this area. That in itself is a complete story. Kata Tjuta, or Mount Olga as you know it, will be a separate travelogue and we intend to incorporate more of the Tjukurpa – or traditional Aboriginal Law – into that story!"

"Wonderful! I say Payne, have your researchers finalised the scripts for the Olga's?"

Payne pursed his lips before thoughtfully answering.

"Do I detect a carrot upon which I may exert a little influence over you?"

Again Delumi's delightful giggle brightened the atmosphere, which had become a little tense. She answered subserviently.

"There is no need for carrots Payne. I am your humble little leading lady whom you just may be able to twist around your little finger, should you hold the appropriate information and assistance I require!"

Chapter Six

A DOOR OPENS

Cast, crew and pilots were milling about the two aircraft at the appointed time, for the next phase of filming which had been brought forwards to accommodate the weather. Being summertime in the centre of Australia, the days were a little long and there was still about an hour of daylight, even though the promised cloud cover was threatening ominously. The film company buses with the larger gear, such as props, drops, audio booms, dust carpets, tents, lighting, aborigine advisors and workers, had already left for the area in which the next scenes were to be shot. They had a two hour head start and would be well set up by the time the big-wigs arrived. As the out-door crew were separate from the in-door crew, those in the van were already rested and rearing to go! When the two Cessna's came to a dusty stop downwind of the filming site, the director was in good spirits as he noted that all was in readiness for him. Even the floodlights were on and warming up. He fussed over his star presenter, ordering make-up to apply the finishing touches so that no traces of dust or perspiration were evident. Wardrobe too, was rushed to check last minute details. Whilst awaiting sun-down and the deepening darkness to be afforded by the cloud cover; all acting personnel pored over their lines and scripts. The first scene in which Delumi presented the darkened rock, with forbidding clouds threatening overhead, was to be shot with one end of Uluru to her right as she faced the camera and the darkening horizon to her left. Then the films Cessna was to be seen passing behind her just above head height and halfway up as seen against the huge bulk of the monolith. Three takes were needed to get the plane reflected properly and also at just the right height. Delumi did well!

"Very nice, children very nice that's a wrap. Now listen carefully Dears. Scene thirty is going to be dangerous at night in the darkness. We do not want any stupid mistakes. Naomi got injured – we don't need any more – so take care children! Are you all listening?"

Kurt clapped his hands peremptorily, demanding attention.

"After Miss Vido presents the scenario, on cue, as she steps away Lennie will zoom in with camera two as number one fades. Timing is essential! Five seconds only on the zoom by which time number one should be targeted on the departing plane overhead!" The director focused his beady eyes upon Delumi. "My Dear – do be ready on cue with a serious look on your face and the words on your tongue at 'action'!" Delumi nodded.

Kurt Stols continued, stressing the safety issue.

"Now children, just because the falling rocks are from props does not mean they are altogether safe. These 'rocks' dislodged by the buzzing aircraft, can still cause a headache or you may break a limb trying to avoid them. They are set to fall close to the cameras for realism and some may bounce where they are not supposed to – especially the weighted ones!"

He glanced about his charges, nervously tugging at his goatee.

"Miss Vido! It is essential after the presentation that you quickly step aside out of camera and scoot for safety – are you with me dear?"

"Yes, Mister Stols – I understand fully!"

"All right children – places!"

The first take was timed perfectly but failed when one of the 'rocks' knocked the close-up camera. A re-take took more than half an hour to set up again as the props had to be correctly placed in the cradle for maximum effect. The Cessna had to land again. It was foolhardy to risk fuel in circling needlessly. The second 'take' was all clear and Kurt ordered

"Pack up and go home Children!"

The following day, neither the presenter nor the pilots were needed as the second crew was doing fill-ins. The first crew was engaged in filter techniques for up-coming desert scenes, leaving Kurt and his assistants to spend half a day viewing shots already canned. It was important to check that the cloud scenes of the previous night were correctly filmed before that cover dispersed. The half day break was a welcome breather for the two amateurs. Mid-morning found them sharing morning tea together.

"I see the big bad wolf is not about yet, Del!" Justin remarked.

"Oh Justin, don't be cruel. I am flattered that a handsome young producer should be interested in me!" Delumi had a gleam in her eyes. She chided. "I do believe you're jealous!"

Her pilot blushed again.

"We have been friends for a few years now. As your employee – I have to stay in my place – I have to respect you as my boss!" He looked rather sheepishly at his coffee, idly stirring.

Delumi became serious, realising that she had been a little flippant.

"Oh I am sorry Justin. Yes, you are quite right. That is how our relationship has worked so well. I – I am afraid I have been taking you too much for granted. After all, you are a red-blooded male (and a very handsome one I might add) and it is certainly most unfair of me to flaunt Payne at you like that!"

They sat in silence, each with their own thoughts. Delumi broke the silence.

"Strange you know. We do get on so well together yet neither of us knows a great deal about the other – I mean – you know; our private lives. Of course that is how it has to be in business. I daresay a boss and the staff must stick strictly to business!" She placed her hand on Justin's.

"Am I to understand you feel more than just friendship towards me as your employer?"

Justin looked Delumi directly in the eyes and answered very solemnly.

"Yes! But you are high on a pedestal and a lowly employee, who is just a pilot, feels he is out of his league! Delumi – I have always admired you but have kept my distance out of respect for my position!"

Their intimate conversation ceased as the movie producer approached. He was painfully aware that he was interrupting a delicate moment, as he did not fail to see Delumi place her hand over Justin's.

"And how is my star performer?" He asked. "May I join you?"

He sat beside Delumi as they answered in unison.

"Of course!"

"Kurt says he is satisfied with the cloud takes; so we have tonight off!" Payne enlightened them; then announced. "The staff is calling a social dance evening for tonight, so I thought I would book a couple of dances with you Delumi. You will attend, won't you?" He eyed her hopefully.

"Why; that sounds wonderful and yes, you have booked a couple of dances with me Payne. Just see you allow me a little latitude to spread my wings though!"

Delumi smiled at him as she noted a slight frown cross Justin's features.

As the steward set a coffee in front of Payne, the manager stated.

"I see you two are scheduled to fly together tomorrow. It could be a hard day for you Delumi!" She looked enquiringly at Payne.

"Oh, how so?"

"Well, you will be just about hanging out of the door of the Cessna for most of the shoot. Doesn't that worry you?" There was concern in his tone. Delumi smiled.

"Not at all! Do you forget that I almost live in that aircraft during my business life and my pilot is more competent than most? I am much inured to looking out of aircraft and as for the open hatch; I shall be firmly in a restraining harness. No! I have no qualms what-so-ever!"

"It may be long and tedious though. There are sure to be lots of re-takes. I reckon you will be circling the 'rock' most of the day!" He shook his head. "Especially if the lighting is not right, we couldn't wait for the cloud, now we can't have it disperse quickly enough!"

"It may be very cramped in there too!" Delumi mused. "Although the Cessna seats six, two seats are removed for the camera, lighting and audio. No doubt Kurt will be kneeling beside Justin in the co-pilot's seat for better vision during the shoot. I guess audio will be on camera's lap!" She giggled an infectious giggle that had the men respond with wry smiles.

"Ssh!" Payne cautioned. "Do you want 'air safety' on our backs?"

Justin intervened.

"It is a registered six-seater and we are only flying five. In that regard it is a legitimate flight!"

"Enough said! I shall see you this evening; shall I?" Payne excused himself and departed.

Justin worried.

"Del! I have misgivings about flying five when we only have four seats. I thought Payne was a stickler for regulations and safety first!" Delumi pondered the point.

"The seat restraining harness will still be attached and a cushion should suffice as a seat. As they say - 'the show must go on' – I will accept all responsibility Justin. It will only be for this one-day shoot; that is the only time the presenter has to be filmed within the camera aircraft!"

"You are the boss Del, who am I to argue with the boss?" Justin sighed resignedly.

Again Delumi placed a hand over Justin's.

"Do you know what I think – no - what I order?" She peered deeply into her pilot's eyes.

"No, no, but I fear it is some devilment!" He cautiously responded.

"Just for this evening, just for the dancing and frolicking; let us not be boss and employee! Let us be two free spirits doing our own thing and socialising as two adults should. Tomorrow it will be back to business!"

Justin's wide eyes mirrored his surprise at her unexpected statement. The implication of its meaning set his heart pulsating! Justin became emboldened by the words Delumi voiced and the imp within his boyish heart, urged him to recklessness; which was not his wont as a rule. Justin was normally level-headed and a great controller of his emotions. However, this was an opportunity not to be missed. He gritted his teeth, then almost blurted out with urgency but restrained himself with a little effort.

"Delumi, I will put you to the test. Why not let us be free spirits as of right now and make a full day of it?" She giggled in delighted surprise.

"Justin! I knew there was a devil within those stoic features – you're on – what do you suggest?" The twinkle in his eyes gave evidence of his lust for adventure.

"It is a wonderful day outdoors. Let us go swimming. It is a very inviting pool and I have been dying to show off my diving expertise! Are you going to chicken out on me or are you as good as your word?"

"Okay, swimming it is! Oh dear, I'm not sure if I have a bathing costume!" Delumi pouted, trying to recall.

"Now, now, Del!" Justin clucked. "There are ample facilities in this complex for you to find something suitable. I don't want excuses!"

Within an hour of their decision, the two were seated by the pool in the shade of an awning; a cool drink by the ice-bucket on their table.

"Oh this IS nice Justin! Aren't you glad I talked you into it?" Delumi egged her pilot.

"Well, I like that!" He expostulated. "Just for that cheeky remark, it is your turn to break the ice. Go on, into the pool, I will follow!"

Delumi's radiant face reflected the joy she was experiencing away from the serious business and the strain of the stardom so suddenly thrust upon her. She felt the urge of youth again and played it to the full.

"Not on your Nellie young man. If you wish to lay claim to being the instigator of this outdoor activity, then it is you who must show the way!"

"Fair enough!"

Justin sprang to his feet, took a few steps to the poolside and gracefully dived into the water. He had in mind to come up thoroughly wet and drip all over Delumi. Justin would have revenge! To his dismay upon climbing out of the pool, Delumi was not where he had left her, no doubt pre-empting such a move. A quick glance about had the happy young man locate her as she swam with swift, sure strokes to the opposite end of the pool. Once again he entered the water; then swam after her.

Payne Carrens glanced out of the window of his quarters, which overlooked the swimming pool and frowned as he witnessed Delumi and Justin frolicking in the water. He had never seen the two on such intimate terms before and came to understand that even a handsome film producer, could have a struggle on his hands if he wished to win the favours of this beautiful young lady; of whom he knew so very little. His urge to know her better strengthened. More so upon seeing the contours of her very youthful body!

"You were quite right Justin. You do have some expertise in diving!"

Delumi graciously admitted, as they sat by the table, drying themselves, not that much drying was necessary in the warm balmy weather.

"Thank you Del, but you did not have to show me up by doing that graceful swan dive of yours!" He shook a finger at her in mock displeasure.

"It was a swallow dive, much more graceful than a swan dive and the proof was in the mouthful of water I got when you 'bombed' in beside me. That was quite cruel of you!"

Justin laughed. He sipped at his drink.

"Yes! I was proud of that. I haven't experienced one of those since my school days. It almost swamped you out of the pool. That will teach you to dive better than me; you are supposed to let me do the skiting, I believe it's in the small print of my contract!"

Delumi threw a screwed up paper napkin at him.

"Nonsense! You dive like a dead weight, that 'bomb' proves it!" She smiled at him.

"You just said I do have some expertise in diving!" Justin quoted as he tried in vain to dodge the missile.

"I shall have to re-negotiate your contract and scrub the fine print!" Delumi stated. Both lay back sipping their drinks and relaxing. In such idyllic surroundings, the mood was exciting yet restful.

Rested and relaxed, both Justin and Delumi were eagerly looking forwards to the evening dances. They were dining at the venue as lively chamber music permeated the large auditorium. Both were mildly surprised at the absence of Payne Carrens. The time was well past eight thirty before the small orchestra struck up a stirring rhythm of the modern dance. Justin rose and offered an arm to Delumi.

"This is my dance, I believe?"

He whisked her away to the dance floor and they began gyrating to the music.

"Strange that Payne was not in to dinner!" Delumi pondered.

"We do not need him!" Justin callously replied. His partner impishly teased.

"He is sure to attend. He did invite me to dance with him!"

"Just keep your dainty little feet out of his way – he probably dances like a bulldozer!"

Justin hissed; jealously. Delumi smiled.

Indeed, Payne did attend the dances, but quite late. The hour of ten in the evening had barely passed, before the big man made an appearance. It was between dances and whilst Delumi and Justin were recovering from over an hour of energetic pleasure; that Payne put in his appearance and apologies.

“Please forgive me, Delumi!” He begged. “I was called to an impromptu board meeting. It appears that the parts are here for the Cessna and the production costs are well in hand (thanks to the reduction in re-takes) and filming is on schedule. But – we do have staff problems – some of the Aborigines have gone walk-a-bout without notice and two of the crew have come down with some fly-related illness! May I sit a minute?” He did so.

“Will the staff shortages affect the filming tomorrow?” Delumi worried. Payne shook his head.

“No! Thankfully they are the ‘prop’ staff and can be done without for tomorrow’s exercises. Anyway, they are easily replaceable. The Aborigines are a worry though, as they are members of the Anangu and are a delicate part of the infrastructure which governs our rights to film in specific areas. We cannot afford to upset them; especially if we are to do our Kata Tjuta Travelogue!” His face mirrored genuine concern.

Delumi took Payne’s mind off his worries by changing the subject. “You owe me a couple of dances Payne!” She glanced at Justin. “Would you excuse us?” Justin could do little but reply. “Of course!” He sat alone.

Chapter Seven

ENLIGHTENMENT

Kurt's elbow kept nudging Justin's ear as the Director gesticulated silently to his star and film crew, as filming progressed throughout the morning. It was a harrowing experience for both Justin and Delumi alike. In the pilot's instance, the constant elbow in his ear was just about as irritating as a pesky fly which kept returning to the same spot, no matter how often it was swatted away. Keeping the aircraft in exactly the right flight-path was worry enough, without an irritating unwanted elbow. Delumi, on the other hand, was being exhorted into what could only be described as a 'death defying' stunt; by the meticulous Director. Due to the cramped conditions within the light aircraft, Delumi was at the full extent of her restraining harness in a precarious position hanging out of the aft hatch. This was necessary to acquire the proper focus of the camera, as the object Cessna had to be in focus too; in the background. As Payne predicted, they were airborne for the full morning session. Re-take after re-take became a necessity due to divers factors. Many times the presenter's words were interrupted by instructions over the pilot's radio by Ground Control. As this could not be dubbed out, it necessitated re-takes. At other times the odd dispersing cloud would cross the big rock or the object Cessna, causing colour focus problems with shots which were supposed to be filmed on a cloudless, steaming summer day. Lack of correct altitude by both aircraft at different times also caused problems. Refuelling and replenishing too, was an irritation to the fidgety Director.

"I warned you!" Payne said, as he plonked into a chair at the lunch table. "By the look of you two, I would say you have had a harrowing morning!"

Delumi sighed.

"There is no doubt about it. The interior of a Cessna is nowhere near as comfortable as a studio on the ground. I know one has to spread one's wings to fly but a studio wins hands down in the wing spreading department!"

Justin concurred.

"I have had my ears boxed so many times by Kurt's elbow that I am sure it will develop a large callous!"

Payne glanced at the indicated ear.

"I don't think it will make any difference, looks like it has already been calloused!"

Delumi smiled slightly but Justin chose to ignore the remark.

"Thank goodness we only have two more scenes of the interior shoots!"

Delumi sighed, and then addressed Justin.

"Pour me another coffee – there's a Dear!" It was done. The pilot mused.

"We may get another break after those two scenes are canned, Del! Kurt may not be able to find any dingoes with the Aborigines gone walk-a-bout!"

Payne advised.

"Oh there is still one Aborigine here. Old Jack Eno, the black tracker. Reckons he is too old to go walk-a-bout and he swears he knows every dingo in the district by name. He will find all the dingoes Kurt needs; anyway, you only have to go to the camp ground to find those Australian wild dogs. The scavengers haunt the picnic spots pinching scraps, before they are thrown out usually. They can be a damned nuisance to campers but they have to be tolerated. The tourists love to photograph them.

"Eno – Jack Eno?" Delumi queried. "That doesn't sound like an aboriginal name to me!" Payne laughed.

"No! It is not his real name. That is a nickname the Australian Soldiers christened him with during the war years. The story goes that as a young man, he was forever making and selling boomerangs to the enlisted men. To press his point when extolling the virtues of his wares, he would toss a bent stick and shout - 'see, 'e no good! You catchim' this one, 'e come back!' - It was a good ploy. He sold many boomerangs but all things useless, old Jacky would say, 'e no good!' So he got labelled 'Jacky Eno'!"

It is quite sad, you know" Delumi mused "Some of those older Aborigines are very much mis-understood. Just because they have a different culture and customs to other people, those others treat them as if they were imbeciles and lacked fundamental intelligence!" Payne nodded. "I have first-hand experience at that, Delumi. Just try putting one over on the Anangu; they are a very shrewd bunch, I can tell you!" Delumi confided. "Justin and I have also had experience in that regard too. We were special guests at a Ballagalla Corroboree. Those Elders really did cut into the fine print; few people could out-smart them in the long-term. I believe they also have long memories akin to the elephant. They make 'pay-back'!"

Justin nodded in accord. Payne was suitably impressed and astonished.

"You have experienced a real Corroboree? Wow! That I would love to have filmed!" His eyes widened and he looked at Delumi with new respect. "You never cease to amaze me! What other experiences have you had?"

Justin offered a reply.

"She was almost blown up in an automobile and got lost in the desert for a week!"

"Truly?" Payne asked in awe.

Delumi was not of a mind to elaborate and after a cursory acknowledgement of the facts, changed the subject.

"There must only be a couple of days shooting left now! How long will it be before the Cessna is airborne again Payne?"

"Ugh? Oh! It should be ready tomorrow, I think, but it will have to undergo flight tests and inspection!" He was loathe letting the other matter drop as he saw filming possibilities in Delumi's statement, but could see it was a sore point with her. He finished his reply. "So far as the presenter is concerned, yes, filming will be over in about a day and a half. There are lots of extras to be done though for the Editor to be able to leave snips on the cutting room floor!" He grumbled. "It appears the damned Editors just love chopping all the good cover to bits – I suppose it makes them feel they are doing a good job – damned expensive though!"

Naomi limped into the dining room and hurried across to them.

"Delumi you had better scoot. Kurt is bristling and tugging his beard out!"

Delumi glanced at her watch.

"But we are not due for another ten minutes!"

Payne explained.

"He's like that. All of a sudden time is the essence and you are expected to be there when he is ready. I had better scoot myself! See you both at dinner – cheers!"

He took off with haste as Delumi sweetly thanked Naomi and they departed too; for their various commitments. Surprisingly, Kurt showed no impatience when his star duly arrived.

"Oh good, Miss Vido, you are just in time for the briefing!"

He smiled, then waved his people in closer and announced.

"Sorry to hurry you children but we have located a lair of dingoes, only ten minutes away after the drop at the north-east corner of Uluru! We must finish the last two scenes with the presenter, to leave time to fit in the dingo scenes. I think we will be able to rush them today. Hurry, hurry – let us get the cameras rolling, children!"

A tired Delumi sat alone late in the afternoon; having completed her part of the filming contract for the day. Justin was still required to fly the camera crew to the top end for the dingo shots. No presenter was needed as these were addendum to areas already covered. Delumi glanced about the almost deserted dining room.

It was then that she noticed Naomi sipping a drink, all alone and appearing forlorn. Delumi moved across to her.

"Gosh, Naomi, you do look morose. May I sit with you?" It was apparent that Naomi had not been aware that Delumi had entered the dining room, as she seemed unaware of her presence until addressed. She brightened noticeably.

"Oh! I am so pleased to see you Delumi. I have wanted to catch you alone. Yes, please sit and have a chat. Would you like a drink or anything?"

Delumi placed the glass she was holding, upon the table.

"No thanks, I already have one! What seems to be the problem, dear?"

Naomi looked up sharply.

"Oh! Is it that obvious?" Delumi nodded.

"I am afraid so. You do look a little drawn and I think you are carrying the worries of the world upon your shoulders. What is it Naomi, can I help you at all?"

The sympathetic tone was a fillip to the frowning girl. She nodded, then remarked.

"Actually, it is a question of whether I can help you!"

With which enigmatic remark, Delumi pursed her lips and said

"Ooh, sounds quite serious. What have I done? Did I step on someone's toes?"

Naomi shook her head. She drained the last few drops of absinthe from her glass, and then leaned a little closer to Delumi.

"I have mulled this over in my mind for the past day or so, not sure if I should say anything to you or not – " She furtively glanced about, not wishing their conversation to be overheard " – you see; I don't know how deeply involved you are with him!"

"With whom Naomi – with whom?" Delumi raised her eyebrows, wondering at the apparent secret that the young starlet was harbouring.

"Oh dear, I may be speaking out of turn!" Naomi fidgeted. "I could lose my job you know. Can I truly trust you Delumi? I mean, I feel I should warn you but if it gets back to him -!" Naomi faltered again, flustered, unsure of herself and what she was about to divulge. Delumi asked.

"Would it help if I ordered another drink and you just sat back for a few minutes Naomi Dear? Just you settle a bit and think it through properly first. What are you drinking dear?"

"Absinthe!" Delumi beckoned the steward.

Glasses replenished, Naomi reached out and touched Delumi on the arm.

"I MUST tell you, but please; can you keep what I have to say just between you and I?"

"Of course Naomi, if that is your wish you have my most solemn promise that whatever transpires between us here at this table, will go no further. It must be quite important; don't you say a word if you think the risk is too great, but you do have my word!"

Naomi studied Delumi's face again and saw only honesty and even a little sympathy in her eyes.

"'L' will choke me to death if he knew I blabbed!"

"'L'?" Delumi asked. A wry smile with a touch of hate in it crossed Naomi's face.

"That's what we fallen ones call him. We named him 'L' because he 'left a long line of leading ladies languishing lucklessly, the lousy lump'!"

"My word that is a mouthful!" Delumi grinned. "That 'L' wouldn't also be for Lennie the cameraman, would it?"

"No, Lennie is a good guy. Gee! I wish he would take some interest in me. No, 'L' is the big guy. We should have named him 'Pouncer' – Payne the Pouncer - yes that sounds better!" Naomi snarled. If such a pretty face could snarl.

"Payne the Producer?" Delumi asked, incredulously.

"Shhh!" Naomi began to panic. "Careful, he'll have my job! Please, you promised!"

Delumi nodded.

"Yes. Sorry. I will take care; but Payne? He doesn't seem anything but nice. He has shown a little interest in me but no more than any red-blooded male normally would. Are you really sure, Naomi?" She was taken aback by the bombshell.

Delumi always thought well of people until they proved otherwise. It was Naomi's turn to nod.

"I'm sure, believe me, I'm sure. I have the heartaches to prove it. He uses you up, and then discards you like a dirty rag. It usually happens when another leading lady comes along on the scene. That is why I had to warn you!"

The Managing Director of Klotz Holdings and Investments Limited sat quietly mulling over this latest intelligence which came as quite a surprise to her. Used to having sudden bombshells thrown her way in the course of her business transactions; such things were normally sorted out, cleared up and the next item on the agenda encompassed. This bombshell was a little different though. It was a personal matter, a very personal matter striking close to home. As yet, Delumi only had Naomi's word for suspicion. Payne had ever been a gentleman in her presence. But then, Delumi realised she had barely any inter-action with the man and most certainly, very little to do with him socially. She would bide her time.

"Please be careful, Delumi. The man is so persuasive and at times can be quite overwhelming. He has a certain charm and charisma that a naive young lady may easily fall under the spell of; more so, in view of the fact that he is a film producer. Oh yes! Young would-be starlets tend to fawn upon him, with his power and good looks!"

It was Delumi's turn to place a hand on Naomi's arm.

"Naomi, it is so sweet of you to warn me. You know the old cliché, forewarned is forearmed'! I shall most certainly be very aware in my future associations with Payne!"

Delumi fumbled through her handbag and extracted one of her business cards. She passed it to Naomi.

"Naomi Dear! That is how much I appreciate your friendship. If ever you need employment, do not hesitate to contact me. I am sure I can pull a few strings and find a comfortable position for you!" Naomi read the card. Her eyes widened in disbelief.

"This is you? Why on earth do you want to be a film star then?" She studied Delumi again in awe. "I mean – a Managing Director and all – how come?" She shook her head; letting the implication of the card sink in. Delumi cooed.

"It just gives credence to your point. Payne's charm and charisma! You see, he gave me the sob story and sweet-talked me into it. I was on business for my company – really a working holiday – and he did seem in urgent and genuine need. Besides; it was a new experience for me. A diversion if you like and I am enjoying the challenge; you understand now that I would not take your place permanently; don't you Naomi?"

"Does Payne know who you are?" Naomi asked, wide eyed.

"Yes! It came out innocently in general conversation. I asked him to keep the fact to himself, I did not wish to upset the crew and put them off their concentration. I don't suppose it would make much difference if they did know but I would prefer it is not made common knowledge just yet. I have a few loose ends to tie up first!"

Naomi carefully placed the business card in her handbag.

"Thanks Delumi. This could be good insurance!"

"If you like Lennie so much, why don't you encourage him a little?" Delumi asked.

"Oh! You don't know Payne. He would have Lennie out of a job in no time and accuse him of flirting with the leading lady and trying to undermine the project. He gets very nasty if he is crossed. Payne tells you when you are finished; besides, I really do need the job. I like it and the pay is very good. I suppose a girl could do worse!" Naomi gave a wry smile. "You know, at first I really did go for Payne; I did like him. He was gracious and fawned over me – bought me pretty little trinkets – this talisman was one!" She fingered the neck-piece so Delumi could see it properly. "I daren't throw it away as he still regards me as his personal property. Oh yes! He can play the field himself but just let his play-thing do likewise, and zip!" She mimicked a throat-cut. "Finished and in the discard!"

Delumi cautioned.

"Shh! The big bad wolf approaches. Here comes 'L' now!"

Her giggle being infectious, Naomi laughed.

Chapter Eight

THE WRAP UP

"Now what devious schemes are you two hatching?" Payne asked, as he neared the table. "It would appear my two leading ladies are getting on quite well together!"

"Just a private joke Payne, would you care to join us?" Delumi answered.

"No thanks! I don't have time. I was on my way to the kitchen as I have to organize a dinner for the company. We usually have a big shin-dig to celebrate the completion of each documentary. We should be wound up by the week-end! Just because you are almost through on your contract Delumi, don't go running off on us, will you? You will stay for the break-up; it should be the night after the break – that is Sunday!"

Delumi teased.

"Only if you fulfil your part of the contract and have my copy available. And of course, if there is dancing you must book a couple with me!" She winked at Naomi, impishly.

"All arranged!" Payne agreed. "I will be looking forwards to that – must go – see you at dinner this evening?" He hurried off, after his new star nodded. Naomi whistled softly.

"Wow! You do like putting your head into the lion's mouth, don't you?"

She eyed her stand-in with renewed respect.

"I just may see how far he goes, and then if you are right, I will play him at his own game!" Delumi confided.

At dinner that evening, Payne seemed ill at ease. Delumi and Naomi knew that it was because Naomi had been invited to join them. She accepted with renewed confidence, knowing that she had a kindred spirit in Delumi; to bat for her if things got out of hand. Justin seemed all unaware of the slight tension at the table. He sighed.

"Well, that's my lot for the movie career. The old Cessna is back to normal now with all seats back in place and the studio plane is to be fitted out tomorrow. I think all of the air scenes are completed anyhow, so it probably won't be used; after all the hype to get it airborne!"

"Kurt was very worried at first – you know – being untried, first time and all that. But he actually said some nice things about your flying. Begrudgingly of course, he reckons that people expect directors to grumble; but you did do a top job and we all appreciate that!"

Justin was openly pleased to hear the words of praise from the producer, in front of his boss.

"Thanks. It is nice to know one is appreciated."

"Yes! I have just one more day's work left too, if all goes as smoothly as it has been. Kurt told the crew that we could be finished a day earlier than expected!" Delumi happily said, then turned to Naomi. "Naomi! I've just had a brilliant idea. Saturday will be a free day for all of us! Why don't you come with Justin and I on a shopping trip – would you like that?"

Startled, Naomi sat mouth agape for a moment; then querulously asked. "Shopping, where?" Justin answered for Delumi.

"It would have to be Alice Springs. Other that this complex, that is the nearest shopping centre of any size about here!"

"Or we could go south to Oodnadatta. That is only about three hours flying time; isn't it, Justin?" Delumi asked her pilot.

"About!" He agreed. "But what are we shopping for, is there something special we're after?" Naomi worried.

"Since when does a woman need an excuse to go shopping Naomi Dear? We are sure to find some little delight, but it is mainly to stretch our legs and see some different sights. Maybe pop into a Chinese Restaurant or something. Wouldn't you like to get away from this complex for a little while?" Delumi eagerly implored.

Payne had other plans for his new star's day off. He was quick to point out.

"After the company dinner, we will all be packing and leaving. I had planned a picnic for you and I Delumi; on your loose day. I have to take a quick flight to the Olga's and was hoping you would accompany me. I will be disappointed if you don't come along!"

"Oh Payne, how sweet of you to invite me I am sorry. I could not leave Justin to just mull about on his own and now I have Naomi all excited. It would be a shame to let those two down now – besides – I do have an object mission at 'The Alice'! You see, we won't be calling there on our way back; we have to head straight for Kalgoorlie, then on to Perth! I'm so sorry!" She smiled coyly.

Payne pretended not to be put out. He said, off-handedly.

"Oh, not to worry it was just a thought; you go off on your shopping spree!"

All three diners at that table knew he was seething deep inside. He could not hide his displeasure as well as he thought he could. He spoke very little throughout the rest of the meal and excused himself at the first opportunity which presented itself. It came via one of the 'prop' staff! Payne was urgently required by the Editor. He left hurriedly. As the producer left the room, Naomi spluttered.

"Oh Delumi, that was wonderful! I thought he would burst when you invited me to go shopping and didn't he look sour when he saw me dining with you? Oh! This is a priceless evening. I wouldn't have missed it for quids!"

Justin had cause to enquire.

"Listen here you two! What is going on? I feel I have missed something somewhere and I am sure Payne has left in a huff. Doesn't he like being stood up?"

Justin was left momentarily un-answered, as his query caused a near riot with his two companions. They erupted into uncontrollable laughter and giggles, which both fought hard to bring under control. The uncertain smile on Justin's face as he attempted to join their merriment; had the two ladies fall into giggling fits again.

"Come, come! Decorum girls, settle down. People may think I'm a comedian!" Justin sat and had to bide his time. Eventually the teary eyed duo desisted, wiping tears from their faces.

"Dear me!" Delumi stated. "I think it may be wise to let Justin in on it Naomi – what say?" Naomi nodded.

"I will tell him! Justin, I have explained to Delumi that Payne is a wolf; a very cunning, scheming wolf. Delumi just brilliantly out-smarted him in front of us and he had to pretend it didn't matter. Ah! Serves him right!"

"I see!" Justin eyed the ladies suspiciously. "You don't have your sights set on me next, I hope?"

"It could be!" Delumi prettily teased. "I am beginning to appreciate you more, my dear sensible pilot!"

"Grab him Delumi, before I do. Gentlemen are very hard to come by!" Naomi urged.

Delumi turned to her in mock horror.

"Well that is nice I must say. You greedy little thing, you already have your heart set on Lennie!"

The trio arrived at the Alice Springs Airport at close to eleven in the morning. It was not as large a township as Delumi had imagined it to be; and more or less just suddenly appeared as a blot on the dusty red landscape, as seen from the Cessna. 'The Alice', as the township is affectionately known, was not a hive of bustling activity as are the larger cities of Australia. It did have the distinction of being the 'Dead Heart' of the largest island in the world though. This fact alone brought many tourists and therefore the streets were more alive than could be said of the settlement in the 'horse and buggy' days. Alice Springs was a major junction for air travel and a constant stream of commuter tourist buses crossing the continent from end to end and side to side. It was a major stop for all traffic from Darwin in the North, to disperse across the huge continent. The train connections from the Southern States also caused a boom in the population growth, and tourism. It was alive enough for these three visitors, after the quiet of the complex near Uluru! Delumi's first and most important purchase was at a printer's establishment. It was an order for one thousand name-tags for the Ballagalla children. Delumi ordered that they boldly state the tribal name and the city's name, leaving a blank space for the name of each individual child. These were to be left in the care of the local Historic Society and issued to the children on arrival at Alice Springs. The Historic Society was to be the first scheduled visit for them, prior to the overnight stay at Uluru! Once all of her official business was concluded, Delumi joined Justin and Naomi at the pre-arranged spot; a local Chinese Eatery. By the time she arrived, most lunch-time diners had left and the trio had the premises almost to themselves. Justin and Naomi had already emptied one pot of Chinese tea while waiting. Another was ordered with their meals. Delumi gratefully relaxed in her chair.

"Oh dear! I seem to have been running around like a March hare! Don't you dare tell anyone? I am going to slip out of my shoes!" She did so.

Justin impishly fancied suggesting that the soup may curdle, but thought better of it and only allowed himself a slight smile.

"All right Justin! What is so funny?" Delumi demanded.

"Huh? Oh – er—the thought of you hopping about like a March hare!" He lied.

The relaxing company of Justin and Delumi, had Naomi open up and show herself for the charming girl she really was; it caused Delumi to comment.

"Really you know, I think you should get away from Payne, Naomi. To be at his beck and call does not sit right with your nature. I am sure there are better opportunities for you elsewhere!" Naomi looked sharply at Delumi.

"You think so? I wouldn't know where to look; I don't fancy going overseas just yet. I really do not think I am ready for that. I need a lot more local experience before I go for the big time!" Justin remarked.

"You must have been through acting school. Do you have an agent at all?"

"Yes, and he takes far too much for what little comes my way – I mean – all he arranges are these piddling little travelogues. I want to do some full-length pictures!" Naomi shook her head as she continued. "I don't like the scene with Payne now that I have experienced what a pig he can be. Oh the rest of the crew is wonderful, it's just him that is the problem and usually the big banana is the hardest to pick!"

Delumi patted her lips with a napkin, and then took a sip from her cup.

"You know what?" She asked, then immediately went on before they had time to answer.

"What you need is a complete change of format and I believe I know just what that should be!"

"Hello! Be very wary Naomi; I have a feeling you are going to be manipulated!"

Justin cautioned.

"Ah well!" Naomi sighed. "Maybe I do need a change of direction. What change of format do you advise Delumi?"

"Television!" Her two companions sat dumbfounded.

"Television?" Naomi asked in awe. Delumi elaborated. "Television is a wonderful venue for a Professional Presenter and it has a much better chance of airing your talents to the world in general, than a stuffy little Travelogue which people may not get to look at; other than every blue moon!" She glanced triumphantly from one to the other, seeking approbation.

"It is a thought!" Naomi agreed. "But I think that is one area where there would be very stiff competition!"

"Yes!" Delumi concurred. "But one of our companies' advertising stations has a General Manager who owes me a favour -?" She grinned a Cheshire cat grin. "How is your contract with the film company?"

Naomi brightened.

"It is renewable after each documentary is completed. That is how 'L' keeps his staff in order; especially his leading ladies! You know, I do think I would like to give television a go. Would you really help me Delumi?" Naomi peered expectantly at her saviour.

"There is another area in which I may be able to assist you, too; Naomi. That is with your agent. Give me the details and I shall get on the line to him and straighten out your contract. I am sure my weight with the K.H.I.L. will give a bit of bite!" Delumi told her. Justin observed. "You are gone now, Naomi. Once Del' gets started she is hard to stop, just be a good subservient little girl and go along with it; you are sure to benefit in the long run!" Naomi blew a silent whistle. "I don't doubt it. Not for one minute. I have seen the way she deals with Film Producers!" She had somewhat of a glow of respect for Delumi on her face.

Delumi was quick to change the subject.

"Right, that is settled – now – if we are all finished, let us go. Justin, would you fix the Bill for us, there's a dear!" The trio rose to go shopping.

The company dinner dance to celebrate the completion of filming was well under way. Justin was dancing with Delumi, when he felt a tap on his shoulder.

"Excuse me, may I cut in?" It was Payne.

Justin graciously stepped away and allowed the ignorant big producer to jostle in. 'He could have waited for the next dance' Justin thought; darkly. He sat down and watched the gyrating throng. Naomi sat a few seats away with her plastered leg awkwardly out in front of her. Although the normally vibrant young lady was temporarily demobilised, it did not seem to worry her unduly, as she had a very attentive cameraman with whom to talk. Lennie had evidently been snared by her, on Delumi's advice. Payne was sweet-talking Delumi as they danced.

"You did miss a lovely day at 'The Olga's', you know! I had my secretary pack a hamper and we found a glorious spot to picnic. It does help when one has access to an aircraft. A suitable spot is easily found, although we did have to get to it; but crikey, it was well worth while. You really did miss a great day!" It was a demure Delumi who acknowledged.

"Oh, I am sure, it would have been lovely!"

The dance music ceased. The dancers retired to their tables for refreshments. As they settled in their chairs, Payne asked.

"Did you find what you were seeking at 'The Alice'?" His air was casual.

Delumi felt he did not care one way or the other, so she answered just as casually.

"Yes thank you!"

Justin had left the table to seek the company of the other two pilots from the film crew. Delumi could see him chatting with them at a table by the far wall of the dining room. Payne drummed his fingers upon the table. Delumi could see he was painfully aware of the near presence of Naomi. The big man glanced her way occasionally.

"You – er – you seem to get on well with the former leading lady. She is not pestering you, I hope?" Payne awkwardly asked.

"No! As a matter of fact it was I who has been pestering her actually. We get on well together and have our own little confidences!"

Delumi answered with a twinkle in her eye and an expression on her face that Payne found hard to analyse. The music broke out, stirring the patrons into action again. The dance floor began to fill. Out of the corner of his eye, Payne noticed that Justin rose and was headed their way.

"Do you wish to dance or would you rather a walk out in the moonlight?" Payne asked.

"Oh! The moonlight sounds wonderful. Let us try that!"

Delumi rose and they made their way through the tables, passing Justin as they did. He received an exaggerated wink from Delumi, unnoticed by her escort. Justin sought and found a partner with whom to dance, knowing that his employer had things well in control. He smiled smugly. On the patio outside the dining room, the pair strolled.

"Isn't it a lovely evening? Filming finished and we can head for distant pastures tomorrow!" Delumi sighed. Payne held her closely to him and his lips sought hers.

"Do you always take what you want – 'L'? Delumi asked.

Chapter Nine

THE BALLAGALLA CHILDREN

"Hell!" Payne expostulated, stepping away from Delumi as if she were a hot potato. His eyes blinked wildly and he uncomfortably stammered.

"Who – who's been spreading rumours? Naomi! That little vixen, Naomi; I'll wring her rotten lying neck!"

"Oh! I have touched a raw nerve, haven't I?" Delumi purred, trying to calm the producer down a little; to take the heat off her friend. "I wasn't sure you had even heard the rumour, Payne. You did come on quite suddenly and a little strongly – are you sure it's just a rumour?" To his credit, the big man regained his composure.

"Forgive me Delumi; I guess I was a little tactless. It's just that you are so beautiful and out here in the moonlight you look so ravishing – I – I just could not hold my feelings in any longer!" He had a most repentant look on his face. Delumi let Naomi's earlier words of warning come to mind. 'He has charm and charisma'! A coy smile flitted across her face.

"I thought it was just a nick-name for 'Latin Lover'!' She lied.

Evidently the sudden shock of his disclosure as a 'ladies man' put a damper on Payne's amorous approaches to Delumi. He became the fluent gentleman that his outward appearance indicated. Payne went to great lengths to show Delumi that he was not just a lustful debauchee who made a habit of random conquests. For the rest of that fateful evening, he behaved as was expected of a man who managed a large company of people. After all, he was a Movie Producer who had a reputation as a gentleman of some note, to keep intact. The rest of the evening was uneventful. Payne took his leave of Delumi at a respectable hour and it was Justin who escorted the vibrant young lady the few doors to her room. Both enjoyed a restful night's sleep. Justin dreaming of the door opening to him just a little, so far as his relationship with Delumi went; and Delumi? Well, the satisfied glint in her eyes told that she was enjoying her 'cat and mouse' games with the big producer. Up bright and early the next morning the Cessna was winging its way to Alice Springs. It was but a small hop from Uluru. Loose ends had to be finalised for the comfort of the Ballagalla children and their minders. Accommodation, food etcetera, had to be catered for and an approximate count of the expected influx of youngsters estimated for the on-going learning excursions, had to be noted. A week's notice for the arrival of the parties was required and an itinerary planned. When this had been finalised, Delumi once again contacted Djindagarra to notify him of the progress made and to get a firm date for the big excursion. The May school holidays were deemed to be the best time. It was necessary also, to get a firm head count so that transport could be arranged. Before they left 'The Alice', Delumi sent two messages, one to Payne thanking him for the experience of the travelogue presentation and the scripts that were part of the contract, with a fond farewell and a promise to contact him soon. The other message was a private note for Naomi, stating that the promise of a job would be awaiting her and a position as a T.V. presenter was assured. The following week had Justin fly Delumi to divers destinations, which were the culmination of talks between the major parties involved with the education of the Ballagalla children. Djindagarra and his father were sought for confirmation of the sites which would be most beneficial to their peoples as a tourist destination, and of cultural significance for the children.

As the various areas had to be seen and verified as suitable places with a compatible capacity to accommodate one or two busloads of children, they were noted in sequence for the best viewing and safety.

Delumi wanted this particular enterprise of the K.H.I.L. to be covered in style and with a maximum safety level for all concerned. This was to be a feather in the cap of the company and a huge boost for its morale and standing in the community. With arrangements finally accomplished, Delumi settled down to the every day mundane tasks that were necessary to keep the wheels turning. Back to the hustle and bustle of big business and corporate meetings that were sometimes boring in their sameness, but always interesting. The Cessna of course was kept busy with interstate link-ups and the usual business meetings, which were an integral part of the life of busy people. On one such trip; calamity struck. Justin and his Cessna disappeared from the airwaves. It was as if some giant force had just swallowed them up and out of existence. Delumi was not on board. Justin was flying solo to deliver some urgent papers to a contractor and on the return journey – disappeared!

"Mister Jurgen's last contact was at 10.15 am. On frequency 101 at the Canberra Tower, he reported that E.T.A. would be 10.25 am. – 'And she's purring along beautifully' - !" The Senior Staff Member of the air control confirmed, after consulting notes from the manifesto.

"No trouble reported what-so-ever and clear skies."

"Where would that have put his aircraft – what flight path was he on?"

Delumi asked a very concerned note in her voice. The senior was unruffled.

"That would place him somewhere near Kosciusko, just at the last ripples of the Great Dividing Range. Miss Vido, I wouldn't get over-worried just yet, there's quite a few areas where such a light aircraft could make an emergency landing if it was necessary. Parks, roads and the like; we have two aircraft making a sweep over his last reported position and the Police Helicopter is also in the air there. Give it a couple of hours to locate him, he probably just made an emergency landing somewhere or other; we'll pick him up and let you know!"

Delumi hated the waiting. She realised that all was being done that could be done. It did not console her, yet the energetic young lady was unable to do a thing and it smote her heart. If she thought it would do any good, Delumi would have hired a helicopter and searched for him herself. Common sense prevailed, the search aircraft were deployed and their experienced people would be better served without her interference. The Managing Director of K.H.I.L. left the searching to those whose job it was; she went about the business of keeping the vast company she had been entrusted with, afloat!

A whole day had passed, still no news (good or bad) of the missing Cessna and its pilot. Delumi feared the worst. Justin was a most accomplished pilot, his aircraft was always kept in immaculate mechanical condition, he usually radioed his position regularly to the tower and so far as Delumi knew, the young man had perfect health. She could foresee no reason why contact was not made at all with the proper officials, presuming that mechanical trouble was the cause, surely the tower would be notified, but no; not a word. The aircraft just disappeared. This emergency brought home just how much Justin meant to her. He was more than a mere employee, she began to realise that here was a young man who had awakened feelings within her. But was it love, or the genuine misgivings that any employer would have for an employee? Delumi just knew it was more than that. When she thought back of those two weeks; one at Ayers Rock and the other finalising the details of the Ballagalla Children's excursions, her heart told her that Justin meant a great deal more to her than a work-of-the-mill employee! Yes, she even had to admit to herself that the missing pilot had tugged at her heart strings. Justin was a man that she could love, more than a higher employee of K.H.I.L; he was actually a very dear friend. No! Delumi could not just sit back and rely upon search and rescue; she would use the twin engines jet now that her regular pilot and his Cessna were missing. Her mind made up, the young Managing Director swung into action! A couple of 'phone calls had the pilot and his assistant ready the larger Lear Jet for an urgent take-off. Delumi was by now, eager to rally to the cause and get into action. K.H.I.L. would have to struggle on without her; for a day or so at least. As she hurriedly quit the building and was rushing down the entrance stairway, a clerk ran out behind her, calling.

"Miss Vido, an urgent telephone call for you on line one!"

"My secretary can handle it!" She called back. "But this is from your secretary; she has Mister Jurgens on the line!" Delumi stood stock still!

After the initial shock of its import came home to her, Delumi hurried back up the steps and into the building. She took the offered hand set from the desk clerk.

"Hello, Justin?"

"Delumi! Gosh am I glad to be able to catch you. I thought for sure you'd be at a some meeting or other - ?"

"Are you all right? Did the Cessna crash – where have you been – you had us all worried sick!" Delumi cut in peremptorily.

"Sorry about the Cessna – I think it's a write-off!"

"How, what happened?" There was genuine concern in her voice. "Are you injured?"

"Only a bit of a bump on my head, I flew smack bang right into the grand-daddy of an air-pocket – jolted me a bit – and I took a few minutes shut-eyes. I came to my senses just in time to avoid a mountain top but the wings clipped some trees and I belly-flopped into a mountain lake. The old girl started taking in water immediately and I just had time to unharness and get out. Had to swim about two hundred metres and then I didn't know where I was. I spent all day and night walking out of the scrub!"

"Where are you ringing from?"

"Farmhouse somewhere or other – hey, where are we?"

Delumi could hear mumbled words in the background, and then Justin returned.

"The old bloke reckons he's halfway up the Kosciusko Ranges. Nearest town is some place called Kiandra on the Snowy Mountains Highway. He reckons that the place I took the ducking would have to be the Tantangara Reservoir. It's pretty remote!"

"Hold the line Justin!"

Delumi quickly organised the desk clerk to get her a directory. She shuffled through the pages.

"Right! Here it is, Cooma, there is an airfield at Cooma. When you get to Kiandra you should be able to get transport down to

Cooma. I will arrange for the Lear Jet to meet you there. They may have an airstrip at Kiandra but I doubt if it will cater for the jet. Do you think you can manage that Justin? I'll ring through and arrange some money from Kiandra for you!"

"No! I have my credit cards. They're a bit damp but usable – don't worry about that. I'll be at the Cooma Airfield I should imagine at about 1800 hours. Thanks Del, see you soon!"

"Oh, Justin!"

"Yes?"

"Leave the reporting of your mishap to me. I'll get in touch with Search and Rescue for you; of course you will have to make a full report later yourself!"

"Oh, thanks Del, bye!" He hung up the receiver and sought a shower and a change of clothes.

Greatly relieved, Delumi rang through and arranged for the Lear Jet to pick up Justin, then settled down to think of the future. 'The Cessna will be a write-off. I'll have to get a replacement. It will possibly be a couple of weeks before I can get another in the air. Meanwhile the Ballagalla children will be the main concern at the moment. When they are on the road and this first trip is successful, the rest of the trips will flow on automatically'. Such were the thoughts of Delumi during that tea-break. 'Maybe I had better attend the inaugural trip, just to be sure that things work out in accordance with the K.H.I.L. properly represented and safety as its main concern!' To this end, details were attended to at the company and Delumi arranged for her to head the first compliment of sightseers. It would be a week-long whirlwind trip from the cattle station where the children lived, picking up about a dozen or so from odd family settlements for a radius of thirty kilometres. All had been pre-arranged and there would be two overland buses with camping gear to accommodate up to forty children and their minders. Of these, Johnny would be in charge with some of the parents. Wallaballagalla was unable to attend this first compliment. It would take the buses two days each way leaving four days for sightseeing. Delumi arranged to meet the buses at Alice Springs to organize the initial round of engagements for the children. With pleasant anticipation she was dropped off at Alice Springs and awaited the arrival of the buses. The waiting was not to the liking of this energetic young female. She found her thoughts wandering to her pilot's misfortune. Justin was not able to accompany her on this trip and she was beginning to regret the bad luck. On medical grounds he was advised to take it easy for a week or maybe a fortnight. The fact that he lost his senses when the jolt of an air pocket left him momentarily unconscious in the cabin of the Cessna, was enough to ground him. Although he claimed there were no ill-affects, regulations had to be observed. Delumi reluctantly waved him goodbye at the airport on her way to the Red Centre, and he did look a quite forlorn figure as he was left standing on the tarmac! Ah well, perhaps she would run into Naomi or Payne at the Olgas when they got around to that part of the sightseeing. Delumi hoped so; she had not heard a word of the film crew since that episode of her life. Then, of a sudden, two busloads of weary, quiet aboriginal children came to a hissing stop at the terminal amid noisy blasts from the air-brakes. As the children alighted and stood in awe of the big city they milled about the bus depot; excited jabbering began to take place. The minders hustled them into groups and an adult took charge of each group. Five groups of eight including an odd couple of nine, was easily sorted and Johnny organized the minders to take the children to a rest room in turn. The buses were then arranged to come back in two hours after the staff had set up a mini-city, just at the outskirts of the town on the banks of the Todd River. Meanwhile, Delumi arranged for all of the children to attend the Historic Society to be issued with name tags and then shown the exhibits. An hour or so of delving into the histories of the various indigenous tribes relative to the Red Centre, viewing of the Tribal Symbols and pictures of past Elders was an inspiration and wonder to them all. By the time of the buses return, the children were eager to go to the well-set up camp and have an evening meal. As all climbed aboard, Delumi glimpsed a familiar face; it was Jacinta! The shy little girl was quickly lost amid the throng. Delumi was organized to the same bus as that in which the child was a passenger. Although not as comfortable as her Cessna or a company limousine, Delumi knew that she had only but four days of travel by bus. She felt that to experience what the children were experiencing, would make her more aware of their needs for future expeditions. She was indeed surprised at the comfort of the luxury coaches. After a short trip of not more than five minutes, the two large buses arrived at the pre-set up camp. As the capacity of each bus was thirty five, and there were two buses, allowing a total of seventy passengers; only forty two children and their five minders, led by Johnny, made an overall company of less than fifty. Add the two drivers and two more co-drivers, then Delumi; gave ample room without over crowding. With eleven adults at hand, the children were well-cared for. Used to having seventy adults to attend, fifty of whom most were children, gave the bus staff little bother. Twenty one two man tents were set out with a single carer's tent in between each fourth tent. This way the children could be better kept in order and restrained from becoming boisterous. The staff maintained the outside positions to keep busy-bodies away and so that the children would feel a little more secure. When all had eaten and whilst the few pots and cutlery were being sterilised and paper plates properly disposed of in the separate fire of the bus drivers, another camp fire especially set up in the middle of camp for the children; ensured their attention. An evening of singing and stories was organized for about one hour, by which time most of the tired but happy and enthralled youngsters would be too worn out to be any trouble and would take to their tents happily and without fuss. Delumi was just as enthralled as the children when the minders reminded their charges of the things they had seen and other tribal customs that they had heard about. With the promise of what may be in store for the next day – 'so get a good night's sleep so you will be rested and eager to go in the morning'. There was no child who was not ready for bed and keen for the events of the future. After all of the charges were abed and dreaming of new horizons tomorrow; Delumi and the other adults settled about the dying embers with a cup of steaming beverage each, to have a relaxing hour before they too had to bed down.

"Tomorrow's itinery is for a tour of the city and suburbs in the morning, and then it is onwards to Ewaninga. What time do we leave 'The Alice' for there, Delumi?" One of the carers asked.

"One O'clock!" Johnny answered for her. Delumi nodded.

"Yes. It is four hundred and fifty kilometres to Uluru from here and our timetable allows us two hundred kilometres after Ewaninga. That's so the children won't have continuous bus travel all the time. They were really worn out with the long drive here and going home will be no better, so I thought we should break the intervening four days down as much as possible!"

"Yes, that is good thinking!" The young carer agreed. "I have two boys, six and eight, and they can get cranky on long drives!"

"I'm sorry; I don't think we have met have we?" Delumi asked.

The aboriginal lady became shy.

"No Miss Vido!"

"Oh! Sorry, that's Maridakk Goondawon – just call her 'Mary' – she comes from twenty kilometres south of our station. Her kids go to the same school as most of the Station kids!" Johnny introduced her. Delumi smiled, and then asked.

"Are all of these children from the same school?"

Mary shook her head slightly, embarrassed at being involved in a conversation with 'The big lady white boss' who was paying for her children's adventure.

Johnny once again answered for her.

"Nah! The State School only hold about sixty nippers an' most of them are from the Station. Argh, I reckon about thirty – thirty five; ay? Some of the older boys an' coupla girls go to the Technical School, about five or six. There are a lot of correspondence courses!"

As they lapsed into a quiet peaceful silence, just enjoying the outdoors and the balmy summer evening, Delumi asked of Johnny.

"I believe I saw Jacinta amongst the children in the lead bus. Did her parents come along?"

"No! She is one of the mothers in the main house. Jenny is her mum's name an' she has to help feed the stockmen when they get back. She's got her hands full with that lot. Nah! Jacinta's on her own but she's being cared for by Marindakk, ay?"

"Well, I'm off to bed – see you all in the morning!" Delumi left.

Chapter Ten

ULURU

The tour of the suburbs around the township of Alice Springs was over almost before it began. Although the central Australian township was spreading, it was yet still not overlarge. A few points of historic interest were made known to the travellers, but they were soon accounted for and the buses left the dead centre and made their ways onwards to the Ewaninga Rock Carvings, of an ancient culture. It was decided that they would get to Ewaninga before lunch, seeing it was just a short trip and the tour of Alice Springs ended early.

"One o'clock we get to the rock carvings for lunch!" Johnny announced. "We not having lunch first. All of you people stay at camp until the tour guide says it's time to tour – is that understood?"

He announced it in both English and the native dialect; to be sure he was obeyed. An hour later they arrived at a campsite just away from their first destination. All disembarked and the keen children were full of high spirits as they really had done nothing energetic so far. Lunch could not come soon enough for the majority of them. The leaders organized activities for the children to use up some of their surplus energy. Boomerang throwing contests for the older males and the young ones learning how to find lizards in the dry climate. A few of the boys in their mid-teens were practicing dancing for the next time a corroboree was on the agenda. Delumi was at a loose end, so she offered to assist the drivers with the lunches. They insisted that all was in hand but at her persistence, allowed that it would help if she got to work making sandwiches for the hungry children. Doing something useful was very satisfying and Delumi mixed with the four drivers and made light work of preparing the meal. Soon all were accounted for and the children were settled in their various groups, enjoying the prepared sandwiches and soft drinks provided by the K.H.I.L. whilst the youngsters were eating, Johnny stressed that all of the people should keep in their groups and obey the guides implicitly. There was to be no running about and all were to remain orderly and listen carefully to what the leaders instructed them to do, for the benefit of all. There were to be no laggers and 'look but don't touch' was to be strictly adhered to. These rock carvings were amongst the earliest known works of their ancestors and were to be revered. They were unlike any previous works by indigenous peoples that the children had ever before witnessed. New gods and totems some steeped in mystery of an ancient culture that most had never before heard of, much less seen. But then, the majority of these children were only aware of the works done by the elders of their own tribes. Everything, even the most common of Australian Aboriginal Artefacts, was new to them and some of the bark paintings at the Historic Society were an eye-opener for them. The guides whetted their appetites for knowledge when they told of what could be expected at the Arts and Crafts at Maruka, near The Rock! As camp was already set up at Euwaninga, it was decided to let the children have some free time while the early evening meal was being prepared. Most of the children were too tired for any physical activity in the stifling heat, so most opted for board games or reading matter provided by the bus captains. An early tea was arranged as there was a long journey of over two hundred kilometres on the next step to an interim camp for the night, before the remaining two hundred and fifty kilometres to Uluru was undertaken. Delumi found she only got in the way of the orderly staff in preparing the meals, so she opted to not bother them again by trying to help. She got to wandering amongst the various groups of children, striking up an occasional shy conversation here and there. Quite unexpectedly, Delumi came across the diminutive form of Jacinta. The little girl was on her own sitting behind a rock in the shade. Delumi got on her haunches beside her, and then noticed that Jacinta had been crying.

"Oh dear what's the matter Jacinta, is it the heat?"

The girl shook her head, tucking her head into her chest.

"Did you hurt yourself?" Delumi persisted.

Again there was but a bare shake of the head.

"What is it then, dear?"

Jacinta wiped her forearm across the tears, and then looked up at Delumi, a hurt expression upon her face.

"It's that big boy, Bukka. He pushes me!"

"Oh, I see. Did you make faces at him?" Again Jacinta slowly shook her head.

"I didn't do anything – he just pushes in and I have to stand back!"

"Bukka – I don't know him dear. Is he from the station?"

"No, but he goes to my school; he's a bully!" Jacinta began crying again.

Delumi sympathised, brushing aside a wisp of hair off Jacinta's face.

"Do you know what I think?" Delumi asked, then without waiting for an answer, continued.

"I think you and I should see if Missus Goondawon will let me take you to one of the buses. I have something very special there that I have been keeping for a rainy day!"

Jacinta looked up sharply.

"But it isn't a rainy day – there hasn't been rain for ages!"

Delumi smiled.

"Oh, it's just an expression. Keeping something for a rainy day is like saying you are saving something for a special occasion. I really think this is one of those occasions. Come on – are you coming?" She stood and held out her hand in anticipation.

Jacinta quickly arose and reached into the friendly clasp of the white lady's hand. They found Marindak Goondawon overseeing a group of youngsters imbued in a game of Ludo.

"There's that bully Bukka!" Jacinta whispered, hiding behind Delumi.

"Just ignore him Jacinta; he is playing quietly with the others!" Then to Marindak.

"Is it all right for Jacinta to accompany me to one of the buses for a minute, I have something to show her?"

With a very toothy grin, the carer gave her consent, surprised that the 'boss lady' should ask. They headed for the bus. Having reclaimed her handbag from the compartment of the bus allotted to her by the driver, Delumi soon had her key ring in hand. Jacinta watched in wonder as the keys rattled when they were placed upon the seat. Her big round eyes looked to Delumi as she was given an amulet from the cluster upon the key ring.

"Now what do you think of that?" The pale blue eyes of Delumi smiled down upon her. Jacinta gasped in awe as she beheld the prized keepsake.

"That should make you smile dear, it is a very special good luck charm and quite expensive too, it has always been lucky for me; now maybe your luck will change and you will always look on the bright side."

Delumi found a bit of ribbon that she had in her handbag and attached it to the talisman, which was then loosely fastened about the little girl's wrist. Jacinta studied the amulet. It was only small but was fashioned in solid silver in the image of a Koala Bear. The eyes were made of two bright red rubies and it was heavily carved. The dark eyes looked to Delumi and the happiness of the child was very evident.

"Is it for me - to keep – my very own?"

"Yes dear, all your very own. Now you look after that good luck charm and it will look after you. Are you happy now – no more tears?"

The radiant face of the girl was ample reward for Delumi and Jacinta gave the piece upon her wrist a gentle kiss. The child skipped away happily, her sadness at being bullied by Bukka forgotten.

The evening meal was announced ready and all made their ways to the buses, which gave a little shelter from the warm evening breezes. The cooking ranges were set aside from the vehicles and the trestles upon which the meals were prepared; in between. The milling children with carers calling for order here and there soon had heaped paper plates of food and took them away from underfoot and ate in small groups here and there. It was about an hour later that the area was declared pristine again and the two buses left for the next phase of the journey. Most were asleep in their seats when the mid-trip stop was reached. It was nearing nine in the evening and the youngsters had sung themselves into slumber land. It had been a very full day for them and the carers let the children be while the camp was set up. In very short order they were awoken and made to get themselves ready for bed. The portable toilets were a must and the temporary bath-tent was in full use for a sponge-down before peace and calm settled upon the portable community. The adults too, were tired and not long in following and getting abed. Delumi lay in her quarters thinking of how things were turning out. The youngsters appeared to be having a good time, the buses were mechanically sound and everything was going smoothly and according to plan. Her mind reverted to an impish little face, it was that of Jacinta. My, how it was transformed from a sad and unhappy, tear-streaked and forlorn little bundle, to a bright smiling but coy, happy and energetic vision of radiance, by a small talisman; only Delumi was aware of and cherished. How that simple act of kindness was to become a life-saver, was yet to be realised.

The clear summer morning of the next day had all in fine spirits. As the two buses purred along the highway the throng was induced to sing and be happy. The staff were very adept at this entertaining and in the bus in which Delumi was a passenger, the co-driver was a dab hand at playing the guitar. Common music of the day as listened to on the television, which was known to most of the passengers, kept the children in a community-singing mood and the kilometres were being eaten up accordingly. It was lunch time when they arrived in the vicinity of Uluru, noticeable long before the trippers got there; the large monolith was an awe inspiring sight. Many were the tales told to the children of previous visits, the dangers to be aware of and the pitfalls to be avoided. There was to be no climbing of the rock for them this trip as the safety factor had to be upheld. There was a maximum distance they could climb to just the first of the landing stages, but no further. This initial climb was all that the smaller members of the group could safely manage anyhow, and the view from there would be adequate. This fact was heavily stressed and the cultural significance of Uluru was at the many caves and crevices of the rock all around its base circumference. There would be guided tours later in the day after all had sampled the wares at Maruka, the arts and crafts establishment at the wayside stop of Uluru. Lunch of sandwiches and cordial were partaken of at a leisurely pace then the groups were ushered in to behold the arts and crafts in relays, as it was deemed there were too many to cram in all at once. As the majority of the youngsters had little or no cash, Delumi thought it would be appropriate if the K.H.I.L. afforded some small mementos of this historic occasion to them; not only as a reminder of their times of happy learning, but also to keep in mind that it was the K.H.I.L. who made the trip possible. To this end, she organized with Maruka Arts and Crafts, for each youngster and minder to receive a small keepsake of their visit to the rock known as Uluru! These were going to be given out as they were leaving the area, so that each person would be better able to retain their reminder of this visit and not inadvertently misplace their gift. Delumi deemed it wise to tell the kids about their gifts before they went on the tour around the Central Australian Monolith, the better to be sure of their good behaviour. After the last of the sightseers had enough of the Arts and Crafts at Maruka, it was time once again for lunch. The buses had withdrawn a little away from the main tourist destination to make room for any outside visitors. Camp was set up past the buses as Johnny and the advisers wanted a full day for the walk around the circumference of Uluru. Tomorrow would be the big adventure, so the rest of that day was spent by all, at Maruka. The adults organized activities for their charges to keep them occupied and happy. Delumi mingled with the various groups assisting where she could and even joined in the fun and games. That evening, when the children had been bedded down, Delumi urged one of the bus drivers to take her to the township of Ulara; eight kilometres north of Ayers Rock. Their mission was to seek the local shopkeeper before he closed for the day and order fifty cut lunches and drinks for the morrow. The amazed store owner thought Delumi was pulling his leg and attempting to put one over on him. It took quite a while of explaining before he was at last convinced of the young lady's strange request. Of course there was not enough bread or fillings available at that time. Delumi received a quote on the cost and bankcard was accepted for payment in advance. They would have the lunches ready by nine the next morning. All were satisfied with the outcome and the storekeeper was left, with his wife, to get busy ordering enough of bread and fillings. They went to bed early for a busy hour or two the next morning. Happily, Delumi and the bus driver returned to the children's camp. The driver would retrace his journey and be back by nine-thirty the next day. When all was in readiness the next day for the big adventure, only the bus attendants were left to guard camp as the entire entourage were to take part in this, the most exciting day of the excursion. The lunches had been allocated for each person to be responsible for their own needs. Each had a cut lunch and a drink but they were cautioned to be frugal with them, as that was all they had to sustain them until they returned after circumnavigating the huge monolith; Ayers Rock, or to them, Uluru! The round trip was to take the full day and it would be just a leisurely walk, with the special guide who joined them that morning from the Anangu. He was one of the elders in charge of Uluru and would talk to the travellers as a group, when each point of interest was reached. It was to be an orderly, quiet, peaceful walk around the great rock. They were made to understand that they should keep together and not go rushing off on their own. The light scrub of small bushes and rocks were a maze in which, if they weren't careful, someone could easily become lost! At roughly ten in the morning all groups had begun their big excursion. The minders who were responsible for each group were taken to task over the importance of keeping their charges in compact groups and not to tolerate any dawdling or forays on their own. There was a timetable to keep to and the first group did not need to have to wait for stragglers to catch up, in order to be given instruction at each significant stop. For the first two or three points of interest, the groups behaved in an orderly manner and things were going quite smoothly, but as the younger ones were forever being harassed by the more adventurous older children, they were beginning to struggle and lag behind. Delumi announced that the next stop would be a lunch break and all could rest up a little. This announcement gave new life to everyone and the groups were agog with expectations of a leisurely meal. As the majority of the expedition was enjoying their meals, Johnny bade them not to drink all of their liquids as they would be dry on the return journey around the back of Uluru. Just a few sips now and keep as much as possible to last the rest of the excursion. Most of the youngsters who had already eaten their lunch, were hanging about the outskirts of the camp area playing, some just sitting in the meagre shade of bushes, talking. When Johnny announced it was time to gather around and listen to their guide, who was to relate the story of the carved rock in the area and give an insight into the tribal customs and intentions of the various paintings depicted in the small caves and water-washes of the area. Having got all together, a full count was made to ensure there were no stragglers. Then it was found there was one person missing, a check proved that it was a little girl. It was Jacinta!

Chapter Eleven

JACINTA

When it was realised that a small child of tender years was missing, every adult carer was notified and asked when she was last seen. As they had all seen her at one time or another, it was quite confusing as to when the girl had actually disappeared. Some boys were seen to be playing with her about an hour ago but she had not been seen since. A small party of four carers and Delumi, led by Johnny, set out to scour the near vicinity. She would soon be found, they thought, as the terrain was flat and it was too hot for her to wander far! After a half hour of fruitless searching, the six adults conferred and decide that it would be in the best interests of the child, if an expert tracker was given the task before all faint traces of Jacinta's wanderings had been obliterated. To this end, Churry (Charlie) Mungo, the aboriginal guide and storyteller, was notified of the little girl's disappearance. He immediately circled the camp area and after ten minutes, took off to the west. He had found the sign of a small child's passing which indicated that she had been running; there were also the tracks of two boys chasing her. Johnny and Delumi went with Charlie, the other four carers sent back to help keep the children interested in other things. It was very hot and the going quite rugged in the virtually un-tamed scrub-tree and shrub covered landscape; where visibility was not at all the best due to the sameness of everything. After travelling about one quarter of a mile (two hundred and seventy metres) through the scrub, Charlie was stumped! A large area where the tracks led them to was now almost solid rock it was over this expanse that the tracks petered out. Charlie declared that they had better separate, each going in different directions to see if they could pick up some sign of the child's passing. Before the rocky terrain was reached, the tracks of the boys were found returning to camp, but not so the tracks of the girl. After another ten minutes of searching, Delumi noticed a glint in the distance, some twenty metres away; she went to investigate. It was the little trinket that she had given to Jacinta, the silver image of a koala bear with ruby eyes. Jacinta had passed this way! She called to Charlie and Johnny.

"What is it – what have you found?" Johnny asked with interest.

"This!" Delumi held the talisman on her opened palm. "I just recently gave it to Jacinta, she passed this way, it was on her wrist tied with a piece of ribbon!"

"And there's the ribbon!" Cried Charlie as he reached past the bush under which Delumi had found the little koala image. "At least we're on her trail now, there's another footprint!" He hurried onwards, and then stopped abruptly to study the ground. "Crikey, that's bad!" He murmured.

"Eh, what's bad?" Johnny asked, as he too studied the ground. "Oh no, we may be too late!"

"What do you mean, why might we be too late!"

Delumi queried, her features mirroring the worry on Charlie's face.

"Dingoes!" Stated Charlie. "There seems to be a pack of them and they've been here since the little girl passed, probably following her!"

"Or chasing her!" Johnny grimly said, as he called out Jacinta's name. "Jacinta, can you hear me. Answer me – yell out!" They listened for a reply, nothing, not even a whimper.

"Reckon we better look-see over there, ay?" Charlie grimly said, nodding towards the high rock on their right. "If the little one got chased by the dingoes, and this fella reckons she did, she look for something high to climb on to. That where the tracks lead!"

Charlie was running now, calling out loudly to distract any dingoes that may be about. Suddenly, Johnny cried.

"There's one – a dingo – I saw it slinking away from us over there, near those scrub-covered rocks!" He pointed them out as he changed course and ran in that direction.

Delumi was hard-put to keep up with her more able companions. All headed for the area that they hoped would not hold the torn remains of a sad little girl; ravaged by a pack of wild dingoes.

As the trio got nearer to the rock they could see that there were quite a few good places where a little girl would be able to clamber out of the reach of a pack of wild dogs, but they doubted that Jacinta could out-run a pack of them and then have time to climb to safety. Charlie was first to see the dingoes in a pack at the base of the rock. They appeared to be fighting over something in a cluster of boulders. With savage growls and snarls, they fought each other to get at their quarry. Of a sudden a terrified scream from Jacinta could be heard.

"Go away, bad doggies, go away. Oh please mummy, make them go away!"

"Yeharr! Get out of it!" The booming voice of Johnny called.

Every dingo in the pack turned and bared their fangs at this un-wanted intrusion when they were so close to a meal. As the three man-animals bore down upon them the dingoes dispersed, begrudgingly. Snarling but conceding ground to the full-sized humans. As Johnny and Charlie chased the pack away, Delumi sought and found little Jacinta. She had wedged herself into a crevice under some large boulders. Too large for the dingoes to move and how she managed to pull another rock into the opening was anyone's guess. The little girl, with tears streaking her face, was too terrified even to acknowledge Delumi. She stayed huddled into a little ball inside the crevice.

"Come on Dear, it is safe to come out now!"

Jacinta, wild eyed, slightly shook her head, shivering in abject fear, terrified that the dogs would get her if she moved. Johnny came over to assist.

"The dingoes all gone, no more about, Charlie and me have chased them away. Come out Jacinta, its safe now – come on!" He urged, holding a friendly hand out.

The little girl steadfastly refused to leave her safe haven, and huddled, wide-eyed and shivering; hot as the day was. Eventually Johnny reverted to the native dialect, calming and repeatedly reassuring Jacinta of the safety now that the wild dogs were scared off. It took a little while before the child relented and eased herself out of the crevice; she mainly came because Delumi offered a refreshing drink from her flask. Jacinta was dry and thirsty; she fairly snatched the container from Delumi and after a few very long sips; cuddled up to the white lady. Delumi held her firmly and carried the still trembling girl out of the area and they headed back to the others.

"Who were the two boys who chased you, Jacinta?"

Delumi spoke quietly and calmly, not wishing to make the small girl's ordeal any worse.

"Bukka and the new boy, I don't know his name!"

Jacinta whispered, amid silent tears of relief; now that she was safely in the arms of an adult.

"Oh, I see. They were very naughty; I must have a word with them." Delumi gave Jacinta a slight squeeze, reassuring her. "And why did you go so far from the camp?"

"I didn't mean to. I was still running away from the boys and when they weren't chasing me anymore, I started to go back but the dogs stopped me. They were just watching me and I backed away. Mummy said not to take your eyes off them. So I just kept backing away. They started to surround me, I was very scared. Then when the rocks were behind me I crawled in the hole. Two of the dogs tried to bite me and they bumped against the rock and it rolled in on top of me. They tried to scratch it out but they couldn't. I was very frightened they were going to eat me!" She burst into tears again.

"There, there, it's all over, the dogs are gone and you are safe now. Don't cry Jacinta; see, here's the camp and all the others. You stay close with me and you'll be all right."

And stay close Jacinta did. For the rest of the day she became Delumi's shadow, never more than an arm's length from her. They became inseparable to such an extent, that the white lady was like a second mother to the timid little girl. Johnny found out who was with Bukka and the two of them were quietly taken aside and given a severe lecture for frightening such a small child and not making sure she came back to the group safely. The perils of leaving anyone alone in such a remote area were heavily stressed and the danger to her life left the two bullies in no doubt as to the foolishness of their act. They would not let such a thing happen again. Calm settled into the company and the matter was raised at the next lecture stop. Charlie Mungo was at great pains to instil in the group the dangers of anyone roaming about on their own. The dingoes were wild dogs after all and they could not be put at fault for trying to survive. The foolishness of humans was to blame for the unfortunate incident. All promised to remember that they were in an inhospitable environment and care and common sense was to be applied at all times. The excursion continued without further hiccups. All behaved henceforth in an appropriate manner.

The rest of their excursion circumnavigating Ayers Rock passed without undue diversions. All were very aware now that the dingoes were a danger and there were no more absentees from the groups. When finally all had completed the round trip and were accounted for, most rested up thankfully before the evening meal. Some so tired that they bedded down for half an hour before eating. Delumi was one who rested, mainly to settle Jacinta comfortably and try to woo her to sleep. Not that she needed urging; the tiny little being was dog tired from her ordeal. She slept peacefully with Delumi sitting beside her, reading. A shadow appeared at the door flap of the tent, it was Charlie Mungo.

"She all right proper good?" He asked, nodding towards the sleeping child.

Delumi nodded as she arose and the pair went outside to let the girl sleep on undisturbed.

"I need to talk to you Mister Mungo!"

He frowned, eying Delumi intently.

"What you gotta talk about?"

"You will be lecturing the children on the tribal customs and spiritual essence of Kata Tjuta tomorrow, and then I believe you are going to return to your camp at Uluru?" Delumi stated a question in the remark.

"Thassright, when the buses take the young'uns home, my work is done and I return to my people!"

"I was wondering if perchance I might get a ride back to Uluru with you."

"Huh?" Charlie, taken by surprise, mumbled.

Delumi explained that her commitment to the children also terminated when they were on their way home. Kata Tjuta was the final place of note for them, and then their tiring return journey was to begin. As the majority of the occupants of the two buses would be tired and probably would want to sleep for most of the trip, Delumi would no longer be needed. After all, she only came on the excursion to see that the trip was comfortable for the children and to make sure that connections and food was adequate for their needs. Her position as the driving force behind this enterprise, and representing her company, was the main reason for her inclusion. Now that this first tour was a success, there was no need for prolonged management of it. The buses were adequate, the staff more than helpful and prepared, and she could be done without in the future. Judging by this first tour, the expedition was a howling winner for all involved. Other than the children becoming just a little tired with the long trip, all enjoyed themselves immensely.

After camping the night at Uluru, bright and early the next day they left on the last leg of their journey; the tour of Kata Tjuta, The Olga's, thirty five kilometres to the Southwest. As the Olga's covered a vast expanse of the countryside, it was deemed better to witness this natural wonder from the safety and high vantage point of the buses. Every so often the entourage would come to a stop at various points of interest, as dictated to the driver of the first bus by Charlie Mungo; who led the buses through the maze of hills and large boulders. He had the knowledge of what were interesting places to visit and the tales of his forebears, to relate to the children.

His way of relating a story had all who listened quite enthralled and he seemed to be able to make even the most mundane of instances into quite a parade of historic battles and events of great significance to this tribe or that. At each of these stops he would call the people about him and the tales of yesteryear would be told. This also gave the children a chance to stretch their legs and go to the toilet or even just lie on the ground and relax. At lunch time it was announced that the tour was now over and the buses would head for home. Most of the passengers were looking forwards to home and family and the news was taken with satisfied smiles from most but one or two surly looks from others. Delumi sought out Jacinta from her minder, who insisted she should eat with her group. With a bright smile the little girl accepted her keepsake back, with ribbon attached.

"Oh thank you Miss Delumi, I thought I lost it. How did you get it?"

She happily hopped on one leg.

"That's how we found you Dear, when the dingoes chased you – you dropped it and we were able to find you because of it. It really is a lucky charm you know; you take better care of the little koala in future!"

"Yes'm Miss Delumi, thank you for finding me and scaring the dogs away!" She beckoned Delumi to lean closer, and then she planted a sloppy kiss upon the white lady's cheek.

Chapter Twelve

CATCHING UP.

The forty three kilometres trip back to the small township of Yulara took but a little over a half an hour. Charlie Mungo, although surprised at Delumi's request for a lift, was happy to accommodate her.

"This fella like to thank you on behalf of elders of Anangu, for what you done for my people. The little ones learn a lot from this walkabout - we 'preciate that you make it possible. The Anangu like to offer much thanks to you and your Boss-man!"

"Why, thank you Charlie. I'll see that my 'Boss-man' gets the message!" Delumi was duly dropped off at the hotel complex where she met Payne Carrens and made her film debut. Although she thought that may be the filming of Kata Tjuta was finished by now, perhaps some of the cast were still around. To this end she made enquiries at reception when she arrived. The film company had left the previous evening. There were a few stragglers who opted to remain overnight; they were leaving this morning. As Delumi had to bide her time until the jet from K.H.I.L. touched down at about 2pm., she ordered a meal and a glass of light wine at the dining room.

"Oh! Delumi am I glad to see you!"

It was Naomi Progue; she looked to be in a state of bewilderment.

"Why, Naomi – please sit and have a bite to eat with me. What is the matter? You do look out of sorts – is something wrong?" Naomi just nodded as she plonked into a chair.

"Everything!" Her dejected features seemed to carry the problems of the world. She still had a cast on and her leg poked out awkwardly. The swelling on her face had disappeared and although her beauty still shone through, the lines of worry upon her features tended to heighten the sadness she evidently felt.

"I think I've lost Lennie, I got the sack and now it looks like I won't be able to get another job in the industry!"

"Goodness me!" Delumi sat, shocked.

"How and when did all this happen?"

"Do you mind?" Naomi reached over and took a sip of Delumi's wine.

Delumi shook her head and waited. After the sip of wine, Naomi elaborated.

"It's that damned wolf, Payne Carrens! When you left and we began shooting the scenes at Mount Olga, 'L' began to notice me again. Towards the end he got very possessive and as much as ordered Lennie to keep away from me; if he valued his job at all. I'm afraid he frightened Lennie; I've hardly seen him since. Then just last night, 'L' put the hard word on me; either I come across or I can go jump. He's been so rough in the past and I had Lennie to consider now, so I reneged. He gave me my marching orders and said I'll never work again in the industry. He stormed out and left me high and dry!"

"Well good riddance I say, you can do without Payne Carrens. Lennie is a different matter though. Do you still have feelings for him Naomi Dear?"

Delumi put a soothing hand on her arm.

"Oh yes, I still love him and I think he loves me too, it's just that he needs his job so much. It's no good both of us being out of work. I'm sure Lennie has feelings towards me. That monster 'L' has given him a good fright, that's all!"

"Well, now's as good a time as any to take up that option I offered you – are you still interested in a career in front of a television camera?"

She cast a critical eye at Naomi, who seemed to suddenly realize that she had another choice.

"Oh! I wasn't sure you really meant it, but yes, that would be a blessing if you could actually swing it – can you?" Naomi looked wide eyed at her saviour.

"Of course I can. Just you lunch with me, then I think you had better find Lennie and tell him what your plans are; there might even be a position for him too, then meet me on the tarmac at 2pm. and you may come back with me in the company jet; how's that?"

Visibly brightened, Naomi answered.

"Really?"

Delumi nodded.

"Bring Lennie too, if that can be arranged!"

"Oh!" Naomi gasped. "It's too late for that. Lennie left with the rest of the crew yesterday. They have to meet in Adelaide at the studio headquarters for a briefing on the next feature and for a renewal of contracts. I hope I can reach Lennie before he re-signs. 'L' is very keen to have the contracts made solid before he starts shooting!"

Delumi called to the waiter.

"Garcon." He quickly attended her.

"Yus Modom!"

"I wish to make a telephone call to Adelaide please!"

The waiter bowed, then beckoned his assistant bring a hand set. He plugged it in at a nearby terminal, and then having checked it was functioning properly, passed the instrument to Delumi's table.

"At your service Modom!"

Delumi acknowledged the waiter and passed the telephone to Naomi.

"Do you have the number?"

"Of course, it's like ringing home!"

After waiting a little, Naomi got through to the camera crew's quarters. Lennie was not in the building as yet. She left a message that before signing a contract, he should await word from the K.H.I.L. That should sound imposing enough for him to at least bide his time. There was no mention of herself involved. 'L' could very well be informed of the message.

After having lunched; right on the dot of two o'clock the twin engines jet touched down at the airstrip. Delumi had to wait for a few minutes before Naomi showed up, escorted by the boy who had to carry her bags. Still having to use the crutches, Naomi found it difficult to manage her own luggage. Within fifteen minutes they were airborne and on their way to Adelaide.

"Oh, isn't this exciting? A private jet all to ourselves!" Naomi gushed.

"It gets a bit mundane after awhile, especially when one has to attend corporate meetings and study new prospects of mining leases and such!" Delumi sighed. "One tends not to notice the beauty of the landscape when going from one contract to another. More often than not one is immersed in contractual matters; there does not seem to be time to look around!"

Naomi pursed her lips and gave a wry smile.

"I guess we small mortals who are earthbound, just do not know the way of big business with all of its multi-million dollar hang-ups!"

Delumi smiled.

"Oh, I am sorry Naomi, I did not mean to sound snooty or stuck-up; but it can be irksome and boring when one is constantly commuting." The flight to Adelaide seemed to take no time at all for Naomi, she and her new benefactor had much to discuss and Payne Carrens name often cropped up. Naomi appeared to have a new zest for life. Her future in the world of television seemed assured and with the possibility of her boy-friend Lennie being included, gave her a peace of mind that she had long yearned for. All too soon, the jet touched down at the Adelaide Aerodrome and the saga of Uluru was behind them.

Delumi got back into the swing of things just as if she had not been away for four or five days. She rang her General Manager friend from the television studios and arranged for Naomi to have a screen test as a presenter; also Delumi got a promise of a cameraman position for Lennie; if he was up to scratch. With still a week or so to go, Justin was given light duties as an inter-house courier until his appointment with the aircraft medic to get the all-clear go ahead, to fly again. Delumi once more got into the thick of the fray with her business dealings. Everything was beginning to settle down again. The initial outing for the Ballagalla youngsters had been a huge success and future trips were to go ahead without recourse to the K.H.I.L. for guidance. That lease of land over which the Ballagallas had given the K.H.I.L. permission to allow mining, of which the tribe would benefit, had been settled amicably to the good of all parties. Thurston Klotz was duly accredited with the submission and his remains had been returned home and properly laid to rest, with an appropriate memorial for his relatives as a remembrance. The telephone on her desk rang. It was Maureen Darnell, her secretary, in the next room.

"Er, Delumi, there is a Miss Naomi Progue in the foyer. She requests an interview, would not say what her business was but she insists you will see her. Shall I tell her you're busy?"

"Oh no Maureen, send her in – I wanted to catch up with her; thank you!"

"Wow! It's like getting into Fort Knox. Gee, what a large organization you have here; I bet 'L' has no idea how fortunate he was that you bothered with him!" Naomi stated, awe in her voice. Delumi rose and offered Naomi a seat.

"Yes, I guess he did catch me at the right moment at that!"

Through her intercom, Delumi notified Maureen that she required fifteen minutes un-interrupted.

"Yes Miss Vido." Came clearly back.

After settling herself, she looked expectantly to Naomi.

"Well, what has eventuated? Did you find the position to your satisfaction?"

"Gee. I really don't know yet, but it does look promising. I have had my screen test and the director seemed happy – I won't know for a day or so – they want angles and to listen to my diction so I can be analysed; but it is looking good!"

"Good for you Naomi, and what of Lennie; did he get accepted?"

Naomi nodded.

"Yes, he evidently came at a good time and his indoor camera experience seems to be just what they want when they want it.

Appears studio camera crews are settled but because of some new show that is being promoted, they need extra crew. Lennie seems to fit the bill to a nicety. He said to me, 'Thank goodness, I'm glad to get away from that grumpy Carrens. Will you thank Miss Vido for me'; so here I am to thank you Delumi!"

Her pale eyes sparkled as Delumi happily recalled her dealings with the big travelogue producer.

"Yes! He's in for a bit of a shock with his main presenter and a good cameraman missing from his sets – I'd love to see his face when he finds out!" Naomi giggled. "He is probably ranting and raving over Lennie right now. I mean, he has fired me but my stand-in is only an amateur anyway. He is really going to be in strife getting another cameraman of Lennie's ability, serves the big galoot right!"

"Now you keep in touch Naomi, I want to hear you are settled in and that both of you are doing well. Promise me that you will let me know if anything goes amiss, won't you?"

Naomi arose.

"Thanks once again Delumi, yes, I'll keep in touch!"

"Sorry to rush you off, but I am very busy!" Delumi ushered Naomi to the door.

When she was in the quiet of her office without interruption, Delumi let her thoughts stray to that hectic week and a bit at the busy studios in Central Australia. Payne was not worth her thoughts; however there was one in whom she really showed an interest. That one was her pilot, Justin Jurgens!"

Delumi found herself thinking more and more of that time in Central Australia. The dancing and frolicking in the pool were no small part of her thoughts. It was a wonderful time and those precious moments when the two of them let their hair down and became just two people having a ball, instead of employer and employee, gave her a warm feeling. Delumi decided that she must make more opportunities come forth, where she and Justin may be able to socialise a little more freely. To this end, Delumi mentally noted that at the very next meeting with her pilot, she would make a firm commitment. Just before finishing for the day, Justin contacted her.

"Ah Delumi, I have been informed by the safety authorities that my 'all clear' will be granted in two days. When will the replacement Cessna be available?"

"Just one moment Justin, I will check!" Delumi called Maureen via the intercom. "It is already at the base with the Lear Jet; it came last night!"

A whistle of exhaled air escaped Justin's lips.

"Wow! They were prompt – must have needed the sale!" He exclaimed.

"Justin, are you free tomorrow evening?" Delumi seemed mellowed.

"Yes, why, do you want for me to work overtime? I am on the nine to five shift at the moment"

"Nothing to do with the company – this is a private matter – reminiscent of Uluru!"

She waited, tongue in cheek. Silence greeted her last remark, evidently its import being analysed.

"That, er, that sounds inviting; and exciting!" Justin's heart began to thump.

"I enjoyed our times at 'The Rock', so I imagined we could do it again. Are you interested?"

"My word I am. Will I call for you at eight p.m.?"

"No!" Delumi deliberated. "Shall we meet inside the 'Cosmopolitan'; I will book a table; then possibly a live show or even an evening dancing!"

"Great!" Justin keenly agreed. "No employer – employee rubbish?" He knew what the answer would be, and grinned.

At five minutes past nine the next morning as Delumi was getting herself settled in for the day's appointments, her secretary interrupted.

"Delumi, there is a most important person to see you – well – he seems to think that he is important. Won't take no for an answer and all but demanded an interview with you; he is from some film company or other. Here is his card. 'Travelogue Studios' it is; quite an imposing looking person – handsome too!"

"No! Don't tell me it's Carrens – Payne Carrens!"

Delumi looked her surprise at Maureen, who nodded.

"I don't have handsome film company people demanding to see me!"

Maureen impishly responded.

"Lucky you!" Delumi frowned. "Now, I wonder what he is after. Does he expect me to go out with him, or is he here seeking vengeance, I wonder?"

With which enigmatic remark Delumi bid Maureen send him in.

Chapter Thirteen

LEADERSHIP SPILL.

"Miss Vido will see you now!" Maureen showed Payne Carrens in as she held the door open.

"Ah! Mister Carrens, all done at Kata Tjuta?"

"Yes, and I have come to deliver the copy as promised. Please don't be so formal, you used to speak to me by name - Payne – surely you remember. May I call you Delumi?"

"Whatever!" She pouted. "Now you did not come here personally just to fulfil our agreement. I sense you have a higher priority?"

Her gaze was intent although her manner appeared a little flippant. Payne motioned to a chair.

"May I?" Delumi nodded. She seated herself behind her desk and waited.

"You ah – you may be wondering what caused me to call."

He eyed Delumi with a frown; trying to judge her reaction. The Managing Director of K.H.I.L. patiently waited.

"Yes, well when I was notified of the message to Lennie from your concern here; I thought maybe I had better investigate. Know your opposition and all that!" Payne raised an eyebrow. "You're not going into opposition are you?"

Delumi broke into a smile.

"No Payne. You can get those thoughts right out of your mind. I run an Investment Company here and filming is most certainly not on our agenda at the present. Rest assured, your travelogues are safe; we have no plans whatsoever for filming!"

Payne drummed his fingers on the arm of the chair.

"I was wondering what the connection was with the K.H.I.L. and Lennie?"

His raised eyebrows begged an answer. Delumi obliged.

"You fired Naomi and as I feared I might have inadvertently been in some regard, just a little responsible, I got an acquaintance of mine to set her up elsewhere!"

"That doesn't answer my question!" Payne sulked.

Delumi thought to herself 'gosh he is egotistical'; aloud she spelled it out.

"Lennie has a soft spot for Naomi; he followed her; that's all. Naomi gave this address as she had my business card!"

"Oh. I see! So you filched two of my important staff!" Payne accused.

Delumi smiled her cat and mouse smile, she was enjoying this bout.

"Do you forget Payne? Naomi no longer worked for you; she was dismissed through no fault of her own. She was a free agent (out of contract and needing work) I obliged her, that's all. Lennie followed, he was not happy working on a tightrope!"

Payne felt he was being patronised and as was his habit, changed the subject.

"A slight hiccup! Seeing that I am in the neighbourhood for a couple of days, I feel we should dine out tonight. Shall I call at your home address or would you rather we meet at 'Sergio's' around eight thirty?"

He was so sure of himself; Delumi took great delight in answering.

"How sweet of you to offer, but no; I have prior engagements. Afraid I am tied up for most of this week! However, it was nice to meet you again; I hope the latest travelogues are a huge success!"

With which patronising remark, Delumi showed Payne to the door.

"Sorry to rush you but I have meetings to attend!"

Once more the big man felt bested by this managing director, whom he thought should be overwhelmed by his presence. His ego was somewhat deflated. Darkly, Payne Carrens left, somewhat like a schoolboy dismissed by the headmistress.

A week had elapsed and everything seemed to be back to something of normality. The Cessna was airborne, as was its pilot and the hectic life of big business was grinding along beautifully. Delumi now had fully accepted the responsibility of managing such a large concern through necessity, with the demise of Thurston Klotz. She took everything in her stride, confidence growing with each successful week. Board meetings, new customers and the various odd drop-ins of would-be get-rich-quick proposals had to be shrewdly assessed and either cast aside or be fully investigated by her legal team. Delumi thoroughly enjoyed each new challenge as it was put forwards; life for her was very hectic and exhilarating.

"Mister Tarwin Prescott requests that you attend a board meeting at two o'clock today Delumi, it sounds rather ominous!"

Maureen Darnell, her secretary said as she shuffled through her notebook, as the Managing Director was walking from her office.

"Tarwin? He usually calls to my office. That is strange. Thank you Maureen!"

As Delumi entered the boardroom, it was evident that something out of the ordinary was afoot. There were six members of the board sitting around the table; worried frowns predominant. Tarwin Prescott was in heated discussion with two of his fellow members. All arose as Delumi entered.

"What is the meaning of this impromptu meeting? I did not call the board together!"

Delumi addressed her question at Tarwin.

"An urgent matter has surfaced which must be addressed Delumi; would you take a seat please?" Tarwin answered, then coughed and called the meeting to order.

"I feel that as it was I who called this emergency board meeting, I should take the chair!"

He peered over his spectacles at the members. There was no dissent. He went on.

"Yes, well as you all realize, Thurston held the K.H.I.L. together with a firm hand. It has been a couple of months since his demise and the Holdings have been running along smoothly; thanks to his 'secretary', (he stressed the point) Delumi taking control. Now I realize that she is also a Director of the Holdings and as second-in-command it fell to Delumi to pick up the reins and be an interim Managing Director."

He looked about as the fellow members nodded and mumbled such things as: - 'Well done and a good job too'.

"However, as Delumi has not been formally inducted into the leadership by our votes; now it is time!"

"Mister Prescott!" Delumi motioned. "For a properly conducted board meeting to be held the members must be given one month's prior notice and the agenda is to be properly advised!"

"Ahem! Yes, well I was getting to that. Now as you are well aware, we must have a figurehead at the helm; not just an interim stand-in" – He eyed Delumi defiantly – "and so I will take nominations for the position!"

"As this is not a constitutional meeting Mister Prescott, I advise that YOU cannot accept nominations. The proper procedure is to put in writing that an extra-ordinary meeting is to be held in one month's time. It is then and at that meeting, that the chair will recognise all nominations and seconders to whatever motion is before the chair!" Delumi stated firmly.

A staunch Delumi follower, who just happened to be the Treasurer, settled the discussion by announcing.

"I shall send notices to all concerned that there will be an extra-ordinary meeting in one month's time, and that the agenda should encompass the nominations and selection of a Managing Director, until the Annual General Meeting; which will be at the end of the fiscal year. Are all present in favour of that?" And so it was decided.

Later, in the seclusion of her offices, Delumi was confidentially conversing with Maureen.

"There is something fishy here Maureen. I do not feel that Tarwin would have come up with that idea on his own; there is someone behind him"

"Three of the members of the board have been very chummy of late; they seemed to be hatching up a plot of some sort. Maybe they have put Tarwin forwards as Managing Director." The secretary suggested. A knock on the door sounded.

"It is I, may I come in?" The voice belonged to Justin Jurgens; Delumi's pilot.

"Ah! Good afternoon Justin. That is what I need – a breath of fresh air – do come in and brighten us up!" She smiled a welcome to him.

"There is word getting about that there may be a spill in the leadership. I deemed it better to hear first hand what it is all about!" The young man worried concern in his manner.

"You heard correctly, it seems. I knew nothing of it until this morning. Tarwin Prescott appears to have designs upon the management of the K.H.I.L. but I believe someone has pushed him. Tarwin is not a leader, he is too easily led." Delumi confided.

"Tarwin? That wimp, he could not lead a choir, you have nothing to worry about there!" Justin was adamant.

"If he gets the backing of a quorum of the members, he could well have me ousted. I have not been formally placed as Managing Director, you know. There was never a properly constituted quorum. As second-in-command, I just naturally took the reins when poor old Thurston met an untimely demise. I thought it my duty on behalf of his widow. I was never officially ratified at a meeting!" Delumi frowned.

"You said maybe someone pushed him." Maureen pondered. "I wonder if it was among the members of the board or was it someone else." Maureen queried.

"Someone else? It would have to have been a board member, it is too close to the top to be an outside influence; surely." Delumi suggested.

All were silent, digesting this latest train of thought.

"You know -" Justin mused "- as I came in by the front desk, Linda told me the rumour of a spill. But something else she said caused me to take notice."

Both Delumi and Maureen waited for the punch-line.

"She mentioned that a Mister Payne Carrens had visited you Delumi – but, and this is the worry – he asked who was the senior member of the board; after Delumi!" Justin pouted at Delumi.

"Do you think that is important?"

"Payne, Payne Carrens!" The vibrant young lady showed intense interest. "An outside influence! And he is the one who holds a grudge. That sneaking Rotter would have a better idea than most of the workings of power. So he is the one responsible for this upset of the management of the K.H.I.L.!" Delumi pondered the intelligence. "Yes!" She muttered to herself.

"Anything to get even, he would even stoop to undermining the running of the Holdings just to get at me for not bowing and scraping to him. Arrgh, the thrill of the chase; well Mister Payne Carrens, we will just see who is to benefit the most out of this little escapade!"

Delumi had the glint of fire and determination that her associates knew only too well, denoted the fighting spirit that would not be pushed aside from her goal of running the affairs of the K.H.I.L. to the best of her abilities. Delumi, having sorted out in her own mind the problem of the moment; now set her sights on thwarting the designs of her tormentor; Payne Carrens. To this end, she sought out the board members that she knew were in her favour and began counting the numbers to ascertain her leadership. The fight was on!

There were in all, eight directors of the board. Delumi had four of them in her favour; her vote would give her the majority. One member, although a sympathiser of Tarwin Prescott; knew that his input would not be so sound as Delumi's. At a crunch, Delumi fancied he would vote in her favour. However, the vote would be put on the backburner yet awhile. Barely a day later Maureen put a call through to the Managing Director, from a subsidiary office in Sydney, the urgent call was from her Senior Officer in that division.

"Yes Mister Downes, what is the urgency?" Delumi asked, fearing a mild hiccup.

"We have a dilemma here Delumi, our board has been inundated with requests from some film producer – I think he is from Adelaide – to oust the central control of K.H.I.L., from the head office there and set it up here in Sydney. The feeling being that Sydney is more the main route from interstate to the rest of Australia. The man seems to have got to most of my senior staff and is putting pressure on them through his film company contacts!"

Delumi pondered this piece of knowledge for a spell before replying. "Thank you Marcus. I believe I am aware just whom is behind all of this. It could well be a Payne Carrens. If it is, I do not think there is a great deal to worry about. The man is just a small-time travelogue producer!"

Marcus Downes was very assertive.

"Do not let yourself be lulled into a false sense of security Delumi. He may only be a piker himself but his connections seem to be fairly influential!"

"Then you do not seem to feel that Tarwin is the head of this push to unseat me?"

Delumi asked.

Marcus did not immediately answer.

"No. I don't think that he has what it would take in this instance. I still think there is a corporate body of some influence behind this. This movie director – whoever you said he was – is just an instigator who happened to get the wheels rolling. I think he will be pushed aside now that the wheel is turning. Be careful Delumi!" Delumi sat thinking after her telephone call from interstate. That another branch of the K.H.I.L. had been pushed to take over the reins of control had the smart young executive worried. No doubt that it was all because of Payne's recklessness in his attempt to get back at her, for what he took to be an affront on himself; he had opened a can of worms. Thinking that to undermine Delumi and put an underling in her place, Tarwin, he would be revenged; had more repercussions than even Payne had thought possible. Delumi sat in her office with Maureen and Justin, discussing this latest move.

"It has evidently surpassed what Payne intended." Justin murmured.

"Seems to me, that the floodgates have opened with a boom!" Maureen groaned.

"Let us not get too gloomy just yet-" Delumi thoughtfully said "- it is only supposition at this moment. The directives still come from head office and that is here; in Adelaide!"

"Yes, but for how long?" Justin asked.

"Delumi will thwart them, you'll see!" Maureen had great faith in her boss.

"First I must confirm my leadership at head office with an overwhelming majority. Then, when my leadership is confirmed, and only then, I will see about this changing of Head Office for Sydney. It is not a bad idea really!"

This reply of Delumi's absolutely floored her two stalwart supporters. They just stood open-mouthed at this unexpected reply to the push for leadership.

"But – but, are you giving in to this push for Sydney?" Maureen asked, wide eyed.

"No! Not giving in, it really is a good idea. What I want to do is promote it and if in the course of promoting it, people may think that it was my idea in the first place; it can only benefit me personally and the Holdings in general!" Delumi sat with a Cheshire cat grin.

Chapter Fourteen

CONSOLIDATION.

"An Aboriginal gentleman is on the line to speak with you Delumi. His name is – oh, wait a minute –" Maureen addressed her note-pad "- Djinda, er, Djindagarra Ballagalla. He said it is urgent and you would be pleased to hear from him!" Her secretary looked up, slightly amused.

"Oh! Marvellous, which line?" Delumi reached for her handset.

"Two!"

"Hello, Djinda. To what do I owe the pleasure of this call?"

"Crikey, you live in Fort Knox? I had a bit of trouble making someone believe you would talk to me. 'Ow ya goin'?" Djinda's voice boomed in the earpiece.

"Ah! It is so good to hear your voice Djinda. How is Jacinta, is she well?"

Delumi was concerned for her little acquaintance.

"Crikey yeah, she's as fit as a young goanna. Look, I got some good news for you. Ya know that minin' lease that you have over back of our place?"

"Yes, what about it?"

"Well, young Alfie Namatjira who works on the crusher at the mine reckons they struck a lode of high grade ore. The company is so stoked; everyone is getting a one-off bonus. I know that should boost your percentage; thought you would like to be fore-warned about it!"

"Oh, that is good. Are you sure it is not just a flash-in-the-pan?"

Delumi asked, a little apprehensively.

"Nah! It's the real thing. Alfie reckons they started crushin' a week ago but kept it quiet 'til they were sure. Alfie only just finished his shift and come home for a week. He can't get back soon enough!" Djinda was elated.

They indulged in small talk for a couple of minutes, Delumi asking after various ones and even the condition of Djinda's cattle.

"What with the drought and the constant heat, fodder must be at an all-time low." She surmised. "Ah! It don't make much impact on the cattle. Long as there's plenty water we can get by with a coupla paddocks we put aside to rotate the cattle through. They take it in turns to feed off the sort of irrigation system we got South of the bore!" Djinda explained. "Takes a bit of workin' out what cattle is the hungriest. Usually the ones hangin' around the water. Well, thought you'd like to know what is goin' on Delumi. When do you think you'll be here again?"

"Sorry Djinda, I cannot see my way clear for a couple of months yet. Got a bit of a crisis to handle here at the moment, I shall get around to visiting though, soon as the mine sends out an invite, I will call in on you. Thank you once again for the advance knowledge – goodbye Djinda, say hello to Jacinta for me!"

Delumi replaced the receiver with a satisfied smirk on her face. This news could only be beneficial to her push for the reins of power.

Having spoken with the board members sympathetic to her, Delumi sounded them out in regard to moving Head Office to Sydney. Some of them had heard rumours of a move but were sceptical about it. Delumi pushed the point, indicating that it would benefit the K.H.I.L. in the long run. There were many discussions in the boardroom over the pursuing two weeks. At last the members of the board could see the Holdings would be better served with the move to Sydney. It would be decided at the next meeting when the board met to elect the General Manager, and the motion for the move will be put to the policy holders. It would then be another month before the rank-and-file gave their blessings or otherwise. Delumi had circulars printed espousing the cause for a move to Sydney! On interim intelligence, it would appear that more were in favour of such a move than those shareholders against it. Delumi was more than satisfied with the preliminary feelers.

Justin was required to fly Delumi, Maureen and Trenton Stokes, the Treasurer of the K.H.I.L. and a staunch follower of Delumi, on a secret mission; the destination, Sydney. These four were to scour the huge city for suitable premises for the expansion of the Holdings. An office central of the city itself as a reception house, and an inner city sub-urban offices block for the nitty-gritty and every day workings of such a big concern, where parking etcetera would not be such a hassle. It took the better part of three days before a suitable vacant office block of the size required, was found. Almost immediately an inner reception house was located but acquiring a suitable long-term lease, had to be negotiated which was to take a couple of weeks. This could be settled by telephone, so the driving forces for the push to Sydney, returned to Adelaide on the fourth day. An interim term for negotiations would leave ample time for the General Meeting, to be over with before the final settlements of the leasing contracts were due. Delumi only had the boardroom crisis to overcome before arrangements were 'full steam ahead', for the Sydney transfer. She looked forwards with great interest to what most certainly would be a fiery gathering of her Board Members. There was one person with whom Delumi made a special contact, prior to the meeting. At the General Meeting, where the majority of those attending expected there to be a spill; a good few of them feted Tarwin Prescott. It was the consensus of opinion that he was a strong contender as the next leader. Delumi took the chair as her position as Managing Director dictated, and called the gathering to order. When the preliminaries were dispensed with, the main topic of the meeting got under way. Delumi explained that the full board was not to be voted upon until the Annual General Meeting, which would be held at the end of the fiscal year. This meeting was only to elect a leader since the demise of Thurston Klotz, to cover the interim months. As Delumi was a contender she vacated the chair and set Marcus Downes to chair the meeting until the new person was elected. Nominations were accepted for the position. Tarwin Prescott was the only other applicant. They each took a few minutes of the meeting's time to espouse their individual cause and to express their aims and visions for the future of the Holdings. Tarwin, as the contender, took the floor first. His preamble was not at all convincing and virtually was a blueprint of what was already on the agenda for Klotz Holdings and Investments Limited. The applause that greeted his words was just a token gesture from a few of his supporters. Delumi was introduced as the caretaker who took over the reins when a substitute leader was needed and had held the Company together so well. She began her sojourn briefly and to the point. Explaining that a move to the Major City was envisaged and suitable premises had been found, which only had to be agreed upon by the members. Also that the biggest and finest lease had been finalised in which the founder of the Holdings played such an important part, and it was giving the Holdings the financial boost which was so important for future developments. She finished by saying

"A vote for me is a vote for the future of Klotz Holdings and Investments Limited."

The appreciation showed by the applause was heartening. The Chair asked for any comments for or against. A feeble voice from the back of the meeting was accompanied by a raised hand. All looked to the owner of the hand. Surprised, Marcus recognised Missus Dolce Klotz. He announced.

"The Chair recognises Missus Dolce Klotz. We are privileged at this honour, would you care to have a few words?" She came forwards and sat in the chair he vacated for her.

"I wish to thank the members for their note of appreciation and sorrow at the sad demise of Thurston. I understand that Miss Vido was put through a tortuous time and she still managed to run the Holdings well. I only wish the members to know that I am wholeheartedly in favour of her retaining the managerial role on my behalf. Thank you!"

That virtually put Tarwin Prescott on hold. The die was set, so a vote of members present was called for. Eighty percent of the vote was in Delumi's favour, so Marcus had an easy time announcing that the members had spoken; therefore Miss Delumi Vido was elected the popular choice as Managing Director of Klotz Holdings and Investments Limited. In her acceptance speech, Delumi promised to maintain the Holdings in the manner of which Thurston had laid down the groundwork and with his ideals as her guide. The proposed move to Sydney was thrashed out in more detail, with Marcus taking Delumi's side and extolling the virtues for the Holdings by such an important move. Having high senior staff behind her (including the by no means small input of her Sydney branch manager); Delumi had the better majority of the members and board right behind her in this move. During the cup of coffee supper after this meeting, Delumi was swamped with well-wishers and acquaintances alike. She was most moved when Dulce Klotz singled her out and beamed her own good wishes and personal thanks for the way in which Delumi kept the Klotz name Holdings viable.

"I am still in mourning for Dear old Thurston, but I felt my vote and voice would be needed at this meeting. You know Thurston thought highly of his secretary and I am sure he would be pleased to see that you are continuing his work, in the manner in which he would have done himself!"

For the next two months Delumi and her team were deeply involved with the move of the Holdings from Adelaide to Sydney. There was to be a high profile offices complex retained in Adelaide, but the main force was to be set up in the near suburbs to the city of Sydney proper. Justin was forever in the air as his Cessna was in high demand.

"Gosh, I should think that I have worn a groove in the airwaves from here to there, I've been over the same route so often!" Was his lament.

During this time, he and Delumi were constantly in each other's pockets.

"Any one would think we were married we spend so much time together."

Delumi quipped, one day.

"That is not a bad idea!" Justin replied, a keen twinkle in his eyes.

Delumi looked hard and seriously at him; analysing this latest thought.

"Not just yet Justin. Some time after the Annual General Meeting next month. There are still a few loose ends and if I get sworn in for another term that will give us security and a bit of a breather; maybe then!"

Justin grinned as he let his thumping heart stir the red blood within him. That was the strongest sign yet that he had of Delumi's love for him. Justin bided his time. He would not pop the question just yet!

The Annual General Meeting came and went. Her tenure as the Managing Director was just a formality. She had already proved to the rank and file of the organization and to her board members, that they had made the correct choice in retaining Delumi to lead the Klotz Holdings and Investments Limited to better things. Delumi was now firmly entrenched and her words were law so far as guiding the Holdings were concerned. Dulce Klotz was only too willing to endorse the young lady's lead on her behalf. The new mining lease had proven to be a highly profitable venture amongst the many other leases in the Holdings that were held by the company. Things were becoming settled and when Delumi received a second invite to come to the Western Australian mine; this time she accepted. Again Justin and Maureen set out with her on the trip to the mine with a call on Djindagarra Ballagalla on the agenda. This time, they were accompanied by Marcus Downes who was second-in-command at the Holdings; Sydney. He was to witness first-hand, the work paved by Thurston Klotz and Delumi Vido! As the Cessna winged its way over the nullabour, Delumi, looking down; was saddened.

"Ah! If only one could foresee the future, such a lot of sadness would be avoided!"

She was pensive, no doubt recalling the past.

"It is useless crying over spilled milk. What has happened is in the past. Thinking about it will not change a thing." Justin was a realist.

"No; it won't although, the past should not be forgotten. I still have fond memories of Thurston; he was my mentor and a good man!" Delumi seemed mesmerised by the vast plain.

"You know, Wallaballagalla was like an 'Angel of Mercy' to a lost and fatigued young lady, who thought she would perish down there. No one knew where I was, neither did I. Only for the skills of a young man who bothered to investigate, there may have been another bleached skeleton found a century later, by a surveying party or something."

"Dear me!" Maureen exclaimed. "What a morbid thing to say. Think of the better things regarding that part of your life, the final coming to civilisation, the friendships you made and that

little aborigine girl – er – Malinka or something."

"Jacinta!" Delumi corrected. "Yes, she is a little trick; very cute!"

"Have you heard anything of Wally?" Justin asked.

"No, I thought he may have been one of the minders for the children on the first of the excursions." Delumi pondered. "Since I gave him that motorcycle, he appears to have gone 'walkabout' again."

"Should that be 'runabout'?" Justin impishly suggested.

"I shall treat that with the ignore it deserves!" Delumi ungrammatically said, then stated. "We must call in and say 'hello' to the Ballagalla's, I promised Djinda that we would when next I called in at the mine."

"Oh I say, will they have another Corroboree, I would love to see that?" Marcus asked, hopefully.

"I doubt it." Justin replied. "We were very lucky to be included in one because they are very private about their affairs. We only got an invite because it concerned our leasing some of their traditional land. They had to ask the spirits of their ancestors or something!"

"Don't you scoff Justin, it is sacred to them!" Delumi said.

Another hour of flying time and the aircraft was approaching the outskirts of Kalgoorlie.

"If this is Kalgoorlie, we must have passed the mine – and the Aborigine homestead!"

Markus observed.

"Didn't you say that both the mine and the Ballagalla's were two hundred kilometres before Kalgoorlie from Adelaide?"

"Yes, that is right. But we have to re-fuel and have a base from which to work, so we are landing at the main metropolis for convenience." Delumi explained.

"Actually, it is more like three hundred kilometres. The mine is two hundred kilometres from Kalgoorlie and the homestead is just about two hundred from that. The mine is more to the north though. I believe you will find that initially I said the Ballagalla's are two hundred 'miles' from Kalgoorlie!" Delumi explained.

"And you envisage that we will spend a couple of days at the mine?" Marcus asked.

"And another day or so at the homestead." Delumi added.

"Fasten your seatbelts, we are coming in!"

Justin warned, heedless of the fact that all were properly strapped into their seats anyway.

Kalgoorlie was typical of the many major towns of Australia. There was the usual hype and bustle associated with a large community, where the mighty dollar was utmost in people's minds and the urge to gather it their main aim. The population was a mixed lot. Amongst the smart business executives could be seen the down-to-earth labourers with their dowdy work-worn clothing and many of them dressed in denim; that hard-wearing durable cloth that cattle people and miners seemed to prefer. Broad-brimmed akubra hats abounded because the summertime was hot and these portable 'umbrellas' were a necessity. The Cessna visitors made themselves comfortable at an hotel which had been pre-arranged by Delumi, and settled in to the peace and calm of a quiet evening; to get over the jet-lag. Delumi was immediately on the telephone to make sure all her appointments were in place for the coming few days. Early the following morning the Cessna touched down near the helipad of the mine, where the main office was situated. Curtin Forbes, the mine manager, came over to meet them.

"Howdy, have a good trip?" He smiled expansively.

The group was ushered into his office where they were offered a drink.

"As you know by the receipts you have received, we hit a bonanza. The mother lode is still looking strong and there seems to be plenty of alluvial to back it up. We are working overtime to cash in while the going is good. The surveyors seem to think that as a virgin tract, this trend may continue and keep us viable for a good time yet!" Curtin beamed as a happy man should.

"Then Thurston was well guided by his own surveyors." Delumi noted.

"He sure was and the Mine Company could not be happier with the decision to back him. He was very persuasive by telephone you know." Curtin was suddenly very morose. "You lost a very astute gentleman when Thurston Klotz met his untimely demise!"

Curtin poked his head through a doorway.

"Grant, I am taking our visitors on a guided tour. Look after my calls will you!" He addressed the callers. "Finished your refreshments? Good, we will get under way then. Come this way please."

The entourage left the building and headed for the main workings of the mine.

"As you can see." He went into a practiced spiel. "There to your left is the slag after it has been through the riffles. Our trucks are working full-time just keeping them to a reasonable level of management. When the shaft we are working now has petered out, that slag will be emptied into the useless shaft and something of normality will return the landscape, to almost its original pristine condition. Part of the contract we signed with you was to leave it as near as was possible to its original state. Just to the right there, you can see a derrick. We have a shaft going down for about seventy-five metres, then they go almost at right angles to each other. We have a couple of teams down there looking for another seam. It is on the right tunnel that we struck it rich. Now if you will all hop in this buggy, off we go to the open cut!"

Keen interest was made all round as the visitors were given a 'Cook's' tour of the site.

"That there is the crusher I presume."

Marcus shouted, for the noise was rather loud and the buggy added to it.

"That is right. Most of the Aborigine labour is there and with the earth moving side of things. They do not like going underground at all."

"Would that be where Alfie Namatjira works?" Delumi added her voice to the noise.

"Yes, you can see him just there by the pillar. He is hard to recognise with all that safety gear on, he has the pink earmuffs. How do you know him?"

"When we were at the Coroboree he was pointed out to us. He is a cousin of Wally and Djinda!" Delumi yelled.

"You're telling me!" Curtin shouted back. "They are nearly all related one to the other. What with cousins, brothers, uncles and so forth, it is hard to keep track of them all!"

The buggy entered a long gravel road and came to a stop out of the valley along which they were travelling.

"What do you think of that for a view?" Curtin smiled.

The sightseers were let stretch their legs atop the open cut, high above the workings and on the edge of the forest.

"Beautiful!" They gasped. For it was breathtaking scenery.

"This basin we have cut out here is almost a kilometre long and a little over half of that wide, and it will grow larger as time progresses. There is a strong trend for alluvial over there where most of the action is happening. When it is worked out; well, even now it is being back filled, but that will take years before we have worked the 'cut' out. As you can see, we have three large earth movers in operation at the moment, plus two or three little trucks."

Curtin smiled at the group. He was proud to show off his small empire.

"Those 'little' trucks look like semi-trailers!" Justin muttered. Curtin heard.

"Actually they are reticulated. They have two, sometimes three or four trailers attached at times. The wheels of the large earth movers are three metres high. Those are very large vehicles and they only look small from up here!"

"I don't think I will take one home for the kids to play with!" Marcus quipped.

Curtin smiled but let the comment pass.

"Well, that is about all to see above ground. Would you like to go under?" He asked.

Delumi looked about at her party for some sign of acceptance. Maureen shook her head and declined the invitation. Marcus was unsure but Justin shrugged.

"I do not care, what do the others think?"

"No, we have no need to explore the depths, what say Marcus, would you care for a little jaunt in the helicopter just to see the near surrounds from the air?" Delumi asked.

"Now that comment I can handle." He accepted.

The trip back was uneventful. They all piled into the helicopter and the pilot took the full load of them aloft. It was an interesting and rewarding flight. The scenery so close to the ground was breathtaking. The mine stood out like a boil on a green patchwork quilt.

"Gosh!" Maureen observed. "Doesn't the mine leave a scar on the landscape?"

"Ha! Not to worry. As we work one part it will be covered in and the natural growth will return. There will not be a trace left, given time."

"Ah well. I daresay that is the price one must pay for progress!" Maureen groaned.

"I believe the mine is worked full-time?" Delumi observed.

"That is right. The workers are on a six hour shift and are relayed. The open cut is worked a twelve hour day that is split into two six hour shifts. It can become quite boring you know; the sameness of everything." Curtin explained. "That little hillock there" – he pointed it out – "is where the next scheduled open cut is to be located. We have had our surveyors look over the land and the instruments indicated a heavy presence of gold-bearing ore there. This lease seems to guarantee years of work. We have hit the jackpot alright – we would like you to keep that as privy information for a while yet – and your company benefits the same as we do!" Curtin was gloating over his lease. "Can't help myself, I do not get many people that I can be so frank with. As your company, K.H.I.L. has leased the land to us, then I can explain that to you. Of course you realise that the information you are given today is to be kept strictly confidential!"

"Of course!" Delumi acknowledged.

Another few minutes of flying and the helicopter returned to base.

"Good, now do you people wish to stay at the workings for lunch, or should I take you to the mine hotel?" Curtin asked.

"The mine hotel is better for us and if we are able to find it, there is no need to put yourself out!" Marcus argued.

"Stuff and nonsense, you are not putting me out. I made allowances for a party of six when I got your message that you were coming. There is no way that I would leave you to yourselves when you are such important visitors. Please, arrangements have been made. The hotel staffs were going to bring your lunches here if that was what you wanted. As you saw from the air, it is only two kilometres away; that is why it is called the mine hotel. Our workers keep it open just about twenty four hours a day. The hotel has learned to arrange opening times with our shifts. They close every three hours during the day shifts and every four hours during the night shifts. It is useless opening when there is nobody about. They depend entirely upon the mine for their custom."

"Let us go then, lunch sounds good to me!" Maureen said.

Chapter Fifteen

AN OLD FRIEND

When the party had dined and were returned to their Cessna, they headed for the substantial home of Balla Ballagalla as they had told Djinda they would do. A group of four was expected to the evening meal, so their arrival at three-thirty was not unexpected. As the Cessna made a semi-circular landing approach, a large volume of people spewed forth from the homes about and the main house in particular. Delumi was welcomed as a hero by these indigenous Australians, for her incursion into their little community had brought with it much wealth and happiness. As Djindagarra Ballagalla was still out with the men and the stock, Balla Ballagalla was left to make his guests welcome. Manny Binnagalla was hovering nearby, a huge toothy grin evident.

"Us fellers got one big dinner to honour our friends!" Balla grandiosely stated. "We bin catchim' many chooks from 'roundabout to makim' speshul feast. Got'im yearling too!" He ushered the group inside and cool drinks were offered. "House of Ballagalla's pleased to see faces of good friends."

"Why Balla, that is lovely. What about Wally – er – Wallaballagalla, is he here?"

Delumi asked with keen interest.

"No – he gone walkabout since that crazy machine come, he come back when next market time come." Balla explained.

The visitors relaxed in the cool of the house. As every now and again another face that she knew would happen by, Delumi got to be forever introducing her party to them. For the most part, the Aborigines were quite shy when introduced to the strangers. When Jacinta's mother entered with another drink for everybody; Delumi asked after her little friend. The timid young lady fairly fawned over Delumi, thanking her effusively for saving the little girl from the dingoes. Jacinta would be home from school shortly and when the school bus dropped the children off, Jacinta would be straight away brought in to see Delumi. Even as they spoke, the bus arrived. Dozens of screaming noisy children spewed forth and made their different ways to their families. Jacinta was quickly pushed to the fore and urged in to meet Delumi. With a bright smile, Jacinta coyly held out her hand. On her wrist, firmly attached, was the small silver talisman with the ruby eyes that was given to her by Delumi.

"Oh, how sweet of you Jacinta you remembered to wear your keepsake!"

Delumi said, with an engulfing smile. The small child nodded effusively.

"Mummy said I should always wear the Koala because it really is 'good medicine'!"

In ones and twos, the hard-working men returned to the homestead. Of the lot, Djindarra Gallaballa stood out most prominently. His huge bulk which was enhanced by the flowing white beard marked him as the head man. His pleasure at seeing these white friends was genuine.

"Ay! You got another one on your staff!" He astutely eyed off Marcus.

Delumi introduced her second-in-command and re-introduced Maureen and Justin.

"Yeah, I remember the other two from the Corroboree. It was a good night wasn't it?" He grinned at them. "Ay! Would you excuse this feller for a bit; I have to get the dust of the trail off?" He majestically walked away to the bathroom.

"My word!" Marcus noted, in awe. "This Djinda of yours is certainly one very imposing gentleman!"

Delumi was suitably happy that her friend was so admired. "Ah yes, but the one I would like you to have met is not here. He lives far away, perhaps another time when we come back Wally may be visiting; then you can meet him!"

The evening meal was well under way when Djinda offered a suggestion.

"Are you lot able to stay another day? We got eighty mavericks penned in the outer paddocks and they are going to be branded tomorrow. We can give you some quiet horses so you can have a look-see, if you like!"

Surprised at this option, Delumi looked to her associates for their interest. Marcus had a huge grin on his face and nodded in agreement. Justin just shrugged while Maureen was outspoken.

"Oh not for me thank you Djinda. Horse riding and I do not agree."

"Well how about coming out in the utility?"

"No. I will just stay in the comfort of the house thank you. I will let the others go without me!" Maureen smiled her apology. Delumi spoke for the others.

"I know that the two most influential people from the K.H.I.L. should not be taking this risk but shucks, what is life without a few risks now and again? We would be thrilled if you would show us the herd and some branding of these 'mavericks', as you call them; Djinda. Thank you!"

And so when the light was barely showing at early dawn, three very raw 'new chums' made their awkward ways with the more accomplished horsemen, to the back paddocks to witness the branding of the mavericks.

"These beasts should have been picked up long ago for branding, but we found them in a little pocket tucked away in the desert. So we are doing them while we can!" Djinda explained.

The milling cattle could be heard long before the visitors got there. They were bawling in protest at the unaccustomed way they had been penned.

"You lot get your nags into that there remuda with the boys horses and stay in the saddles. You can see what is going on from there and you will not get run down or gored. These are wild mavericks and they will try to break away. They can be real dangerous to a bloke on foot, so be sure to stay put and out of the way!"

Djinda went to his men and barked orders to them. There was really no need as the men knew what was expected of them and they had done it before; many times. The visitors witnessed the hive of activity from the comparative safety of where the jackaroos had tethered their mounts. It was a noisy, dusty and testing time for them. For the first hour it was very interesting as very few of the cattle responded easily to the unwanted attention that was being foisted upon them. At any time one would attempt to gain its freedom and often a rush would be made in the direction of the bystanders. The jackaroos were very adept at handling these occurrences and any cattle that attempted such a break was soon sorry it did, as it was quickly rounded up and unceremoniously dumped by the fire, where it was smartly branded and pushed out to the others already done. As there were only about eighty to be branded and this was accomplished with comparative ease by these very experienced men; two hours saw the job satisfactorily finished. Djinda came across to the onlookers.

"Ay! We all done now. They got to be taken out to the outside pastures back of the inner boundary fence. Are you lot comin' for a ride?"

Glad to be moving again, the city folk agreed upon the tour of the outback.

"Should only take 'bout a half hour and then I will ride back with you. We should get back in time for dinner."

"Oh!" Delumi asked. "Aren't the men coming back with us?"

Djinda shook his head and his beard danced in the heat haze.

"Nah they got more work to do. Seeing the branding took half a day, they going to check the inner boundary fencing to round off the day. Tomorrow we gotta go way down south to check on some new born stock that has been needin' looking at for a week or so!"

"Er, while the cattle are being set free, will it be all right if I dismount for a spell?" Justin urged.

"This unaccustomed riding is a bit hard on the old bones!"

"Yeah, we can boil the billy. We always bring a pack horse with provision for the men. When the cattle are off their hands we usually have a cuppa!" Djinda smiled.

As the main work of the day was accomplished, Djinda had set aside the afternoon so as to accommodate the high profile visitors. To this end, after the midday meal, he suggested a tour of the property. "Not much to see." He advised. "But there is a little hillock 'bout ten kilometres to the north-west towards the Bunjil country, where you can see for miles!"

"Er – kilometres!" Marcus interrupted.

"Ay? Oh yeah, kilometres. It is such flat land about here and the trees – such as they are – do not grow all that big; so it's an open view. The hillock only rises 'bout fifty metres, it's not that high. Still, the view is well worth while. Think you would like that?"

"So long as you do not lose us – I have experienced the desert alone and I have no desire for a repeat performance!" Delumi hastened to say.

"Yeah, too right no, I won't let that happen to you again. We'd go by 'Ute but it only seats three comfortably, unless someone wishes to ride in the heat and dust of the back; then again, Maureen may wish to join you and that would make five of us!"

"I think I can speak for Maureen." Delumi put in. "Believe me; she would rather stay in the comfort of the house!"

Sedately walking their steeds, the quartet duly arrived at the small hillock. There was an ample pathway fashioned to the highest point where the promised view was truly awe inspiring.

"Oh this is a beautiful place to view the countryside. I never realised how far one could see by being just a little above ground level!" Delumi gushed.

"Yeah. Well worth the ride all right!" Djinda said. "Over that way there, to the West, if you look hard you may be able to see the dust from the crusher at the mine."

"Hey yeah! I can just see a slight haze. But the mine is over two hundred kilometres from here isn't it?" Justin exclaimed, unbelievingly.

"Just shows how flat the land is out to the West, of course the mountains of Bunjil keep the dust from dispersing and on a still day the haze can become quite thick." Djinda explained.

"Gosh it is hot out here in the open, do you think we should get back for a cool drink?"

Delumi pleaded.

"Ay? Oh sure, you city ones can't take the heat I reckon. We can head back past the windmill for the cattle; you will be all right if you stay in the saddle. We can get some nice fresh bore water there!" Djinda led the way.

Over the sameness of the landscape, memories of her ordeal haunted Delumi. She shuddered to think that she had willingly ventured the desert again. That she was accompanied by an aborigine whose skills should have put her 'bogeyman' to rest, did not erase a little of her misgivings; hers was a memory that would not easily let go. Justin noticed her involuntary shiver.

"Hey Del" – he whispered so none other could hear – "you are not reliving the past are you?" She turned quickly to him.

"Oh! How did you know?"

Sheepishly, Justin shrugged.

"It was obvious in this heat – you shivered – it could only be one thing!"

"Yes, I am afraid the desert is still a place I need to be wary of." Her furrowed features had a wistful look about them. "I would not say that I am necessarily frightened of the desert. Suffice to say that I do hold a healthy respect for it. You would not get me out here unless I was accompanied by a guide such as Djinda!" Justin wryly nodded his understanding.

The leisurely walk to the desert oasis of a fresh bore, took less time than anyone imagined as their guide pointed out this tract of land or that, where something or other happened to break the monotony of the journey. "That there shrubbery hid a steer one day an' we didn't know it was there. One of the dogs nosed 'er out and boy; d'ya think he wanted to come? Not on your sweet Nellie he didn't. The dog nearly got gored that day!"

Such little gems of patter did pass the time during the ride.

"Well this is it as you can see. I will just chase these few head away and maybe we can dismount".

He did so; the cattle did not seem to mind as they had been drinking from the overflowing tub that was strategically placed beneath the wind pump. There was a tap high up out of reach of the cattle but easy to reach for an equestrian. Djinda unhooked the billy that was hanging upside down from the tap and everyone had a refreshing drink.

"Gosh, I needed that!" Marcus gasped as if he had endured a week without water.

Having sated their thirsts, the equestrians made their leisurely ways back to the homestead proper.

"My word, that was very enlightening thank you Djinda." Delumi smiled as she dismounted.

An aborigine ostler took their mounts and quickly unsaddled, gave them a curry-combing and a feed, before letting them loose in the holding paddock. The sightseers were glad to be back in the comfort of the house, enjoying a relaxing beverage and some fresh-made damper.

"You certainly make yourselves very busy out here, but you can have it all to yourselves. I yearn for the crowded cities with air-conditioned buildings and the convenience of the shops!" Marcus grinned.

"What a spoiled urchin you turned out to be. Where is your sense of adventure?" Delumi chided.

"That is what comes of being brought up with a silver spoon in one's mouth!" Justin impishly insinuated.

"Rubbish. I am just a lowly little working man who has worked my way to the top!" Marcus defended.

"Yes I suppose one could say the same for you Justin." Maureen interposed. "You have worked your way to the top too; in fact you fly above us all!" She said with a sly grin.

"All right, I apologise Marcus. We each have our own way of life to suit each other's purpose!"

Having sat for lunch a cuppa, and a good old chinwag; the travellers said their goodbyes and once again aboard their Cessna, headed home. That the mine was doing well, putting a hefty slice of profit forward for the K.H.I.L., then calling to visit Djinda and the Ballagallas including Delumi meeting her little acquaintance, Jacinta again; had Delumi in exceedingly good spirits. She deemed it better, rather than just idly while away the hours sightseeing (not that there was much sightseeing that could be done from an aircraft), in catching up on her paperwork. After all, there was this move to Sydney which had quite a few loose ends to tie up and the new staffs which she had to organize in Sydney, as not all the Adelaide staff were able to commit themselves to the move. Staff rearrangements still had to be finalised and contracts re-negotiated. Delumi lost herself in time amid her chores.

Back at her office and once again into the nitty-gritty of overseeing her huge empire, Delumi was in her element. The change-over of head office from Adelaide to Sydney was the most urgent of her many duties and that change-over was coming along smoothly. She now had the greater majority of shareholders firmly in favour of the move and business had begun to improve accordingly. The few hiccups of past months were very much behind. The Ballagallas were onside and very happy with the outcome of the white lady's intervention; their children had a continuity of programmes for their further education going and Delumi's stint as a 'movie star', all but forgotten. Even that wanton ladies man, Payne Carrens, was a thing of the past. Her main thrust now was to put Klotz Holdings and Investments Limited to the forefront as a major force in the business world. This appeared to be the inevitable outcome of the combined efforts of Delumi and her staff. Hers was a very contented and satisfying way of life; with the challenges that gave just an inkling of risk with her new contracts to be investigated thoroughly. Each and every one of them were to be scrutinized with an eye to the benefits for K.H.I.L. Daily life continued on.

Chapter Sixteen

SAPPHIRES!

"Mister Jurgens to see you!" Came the call on her intercom from Maureen Darnell, her secretary.

"Oh, good, send him in."

With a ready smile, Delumi rose to greet her pilot. Justin breezed in and that he had news was obvious.

"So, that Cheshire cat grin means that you did not come empty-handed?"

Delumi noted, an expectant rising of her eyebrow begging an answer.

"No – I do have some good news but it will cost you." The rather handsome looking young man hedged.

"I see. And what will the price of this information cost?" Delumi went along with his tomfoolery.

"Now let me see – I rather think that because it is such a most important piece of information, it will cost at least one evening dining out with me, say this evening?"

Delumi smiled.

"That is just chicken feed. I should have been very glad to accept an invitation like that without cost. However, if you deem that such a fee is necessary; well yes, if the information is worthy of it I shall be only too glad to accommodate you!" Justin pondered her answer. "Shall I call for you at eight? We will dine at your favourite restaurant and you may have the choice of wines!"

"Whoa. Not so fast, I have not heard your news!" Delumi cautioned.

"Do you recall my mishap at the Tantangara Reservoir?" Justin was eager.

"Yes." Dubiously came from Delumi.

"Well I received a call from the old bloke whose shack I tumbled over. His name is Geuring – Thomson Geuring – and he is a prospector. Does a bit of gold seeking, but he has come across what seems to be the grand daddy of a find. Not knowing anyone who won't take him down – he rang me on a whim – I told him that I worked for an Investment company and he thinks I may be a little more trustworthy seeing how he saved me from starving to death and giving me a change of clothing and all!" Justin took a breather. "He rang me because I left a number for him. Wanted to return my clothes, he reckons he washed them. He could keep them for all I cared. Thomson says that he does not know how to cash in on his find and that maybe I could guide him!" Justin looked to his boss for her comments.

Delumi deliberated, and then asked.

"You want me to go gallivanting around Kosciusko on the misguided whim of an old man?"

"No, I do not think that it is misguided. The old man seems to know what he is on about. And it's not gold – it is sapphires – hundreds of them, very few flaws and all good quality. I really do think that we may miss out on an opportunity to get in on the ground floor with this. Thomson does seem to know what he is on about; I think this is the goods. What say? Should we go see?"

Delumi considered Justin's eagerness and the odds of an adventure in the mountains with Justin. It could be just a whistle-in-the-wind; then again there was the chance that money for the company could be gained with signing this prospector up early, just in case something came of it.

"Tell you what-" Delumi teased "-we shall discuss it over dinner. There may be a carrot there. He is a rational person I presume?" Delumi asked. Justin nodded.

"Just for all the world like my own grandfather, old, wise, wrinkled and be whiskered."

"Hmmm, I do not know if that is a good recommendation or not. Delumi frowned, and then cheered her pilot up with her next remark. "Dinner at eight, then we will discuss it and with a little bit of luck I will take a couple of days off to explore the possibilities of our delving into the fascinating world of gem-stones!"

Justin took his leave with a feeling of elation and thanked his lucky stars that Thomson thought to give him a call. The thought of a couple of days up in the mountains with the love of his life, beckoned the virile young man with titillating eagerness; but first and foremost, a lovely evening with her at dinner. Justin was in high spirits as he breezed past Maureen as she was answering the telephone. She looked up and nodded to him as he passed a gleam of satisfaction evident in his eyes. Maureen interpreted his happiness as a successful meeting with her employer and was thinking to take the next message to Delumi personally. Keen to find out just what went on in there. The very next morning saw Justin in Delumi's office again. He was bubbling over with excitement.

"You may ring Thomson from my telephone seeing that this is official business." Delumi said as she shuffled through papers trying to determine how busy she was and just what urgent business had to be put on hold. Justin did so.

"Well that is organised. He was about to leave, so we caught him in time. He said time means nothing to him; he can hang around until we get there. Have to bring some supplies with us though; he says there is no food for an extra couple. He just gets by with a weeks supply. Has to go to Adaminaby or Kiandra for what he wants."

"Where do we land the Cessna? Is the nearest strip at Cooma, I don't suppose there is one at Kiandra?" Delumi worried.

"Yes there is one at Kiandra but that is to the north of Adaminaby and their aerodrome is about the same distance from the turn-off road that gets us to the old man's shack anyway. I had a talk to Thomson, there is no suitable spot to put a light plane down near his shack; but he has suggested that the road leading from the Snowy Mountains Highway to the Currango Plains, has a straight stretch just before the elbow bend around an arm of the Reservoir. You would be lucky to find a vehicle on this dead end road for weeks, so it should be safe to land on it. We can push the Cessna off the road and under a tree until we need it again. Thomson will meet us there in his four-wheel drive at ten-thirty."

It was approaching eleven in the morning when the Cessna approached the Tantangara Reservoir. Justin circled the area and spotted a four-wheeled drive vehicle that he recognised as belonging to Thomson at a gate near the straight stretch of road. A man was standing beside it waving frantically with a handkerchief. A towel was tied to a tree by the road as a wind-sock.

"Just as well I warned Thomson about the wind. It is blowing side-on to the road so I will have to make allowances for it. The power lines seem to be well off the roadway. Just a pair and a 'phone line too. Be a bit tricky but I can manage well enough!"

Justin made another swoop over the road to gauge its suitability for landing, and then came in from the South. His landing was text-book. He taxied the Cessna to a suitable tree as cover and they alighted. While he was manipulating the aircraft under the tree and off the road, Thomson drove up.

"Gee crikey by gum, yer made that look easy. I ain't never seen a aeroplane so close up before. D'yer min' if'n a bloke 'as a look?"

He had a very broad grin on his face as introductions were made. Justin allowed the man to pore over his baby and explained what the controls functions were.

"Yair. Well youse 'ad better hop in to me blitzbuggy an' we'll nick off t'me 'ouse fer a cuppa. I got the fire goin' an' th' billy should be boiled be now!"

They climbed into his 'blitzbuggy' and the fairly rough journey over the much used outback track was commenced. Thomson's shack was very cosy. It comprised of four rooms and looked home-made. Just the same, it was quite substantial.

"The toilet is out the back there!"

He motioned the two visitors to enter and the rations were carefully put away.

"Crikey, o'm glad as yer brung somethin' t' eat. They ain't nothin' much in th ' 'ouse." Thomson poured out some tea and they all sat down to enjoy it.

"Now afore we 'as some lunch, yer better see as wot I got 'ere so's you will know it ain't no wild-goose chase."

He went into his bedroom and carried a tobacco box out. Pushing the box towards Justin, he explained.

"That's some 'a the best ones, I got so as I wasn't looking fer th' littlies."

Justin opened the box and looked his amazement as he passed the gemstones to Delumi. She gasped.

"That does not look like a wild goose chase to me!" Justin shook his head.

"No indeed, why just look at the size of this one!"

Delumi marvelled as she held the deep blue stone up for Justin to see. It measured a good fifteen millimetres one way and was almost as wide.

"Are there many of this quality?" Delumi asked with her eyes opened wide.

"Th' place where I was looking at first on'y give a few specks, then I tried this other little trickle a' water an' bingo – they wos poppin' up like darn rabbit-dung. Aw, pardon th' exspression Missus!" Thomson looked a little sheepishly at Delumi. "I don't get to 'ave many females as company." Delumi waved it aside.

"Do you think this is all or could there be much more?"

"Oh they is much more. That is on'y th' surface few wot I scratched up. I dug a deep 'ole b'side th' stream an' went down fer a couple 'a feet. They wos colour all th' way down!"

"On your selection?" Justin asked. Thomson shook his head.

"Nah! I got them fr'm a crik about twenty k's away. Its virgin bush an' I wos lookin' f' gold. I jus' happened on it in me travels lookin' fer th' mother lode. I got these 'ere be mistake!"

"And what do you intend to do with them?" Justin was intrigued.

"Well, that is why I give you a ring. Most a th' blokes as wot I know, they'd sell their mother t' know where I got 'em. But me, o'd rather 'ave gold. It sorta gives ya a tingle when ya finds it – this 'ere gem-stone stuff – it ain't th' same. Tha's why I sorta give you a ring. I reckon as 'ow ya wouldn't take a man down an' could guide a bloke as to what is th' bes' way t' make a quid?" Delumi was thoughtful.

"Thomson. It would be a gamble on our part to take what you say at face value. These diggings could very well be what you say and may be very productive, but then they may only be productive for a metre or so around. I would have to have my assayer probe the area and ascertain just to what extent the Sapphires are constant. Now would you sign an agreement with my company to the extent that we have the area assayed, put in your name and to your benefit, giving my company the right to mine the diggings if it is at all a viable proposition?" Delumi awaited his answer.

"Eh?" Thomson was bewildered. Justin explained.

"Thomson, what Delumi has explained is that if you give us authority to see how good the chances are for mining; we will mine it for you. You will get the full benefit of the diggings and we will do the work for a 'cut'. Then you can go prospecting for your gold and leave the mine for us to worry about – if it is a going thing!"

"Yez'll do th' right thing by me?" Thomson asked.

"Yes. And you can have it in writing. The only thing is that I would like to take a sample for our assayer. Will you let me borrow a gemstone; I will see that you get it back?"

Delumi seriously asked.

"Aw, seeing as 'ow yer came an' b'lieved me – yez can 'ave a couple fer nuthin'. 'Ere, take th' big 'un, 'ave one each. I c'n dig more!"

He passed a couple of the bigger stones to each of them.

"No – no, we could not take them. Here, I will write an I.O.U. for them." Delumi started doing so.

"Aw, I insist. Ya ain't goin' to take me down – so you 'ave a couple. Go on."

His perseverance paid off and Delumi and Justin begrudgingly accepted his kind offer.

"Justin and I will see that your interests are properly looked after!"

Delumi arose and helped in the preparation of lunch.

"After we've et, o'l take yer to me diggin's." Thomson offered.

It was rough going over the unfamiliar terrain. The four wheel drive vehicle seemed to have a mind of it's own but there were no untoward happenings to mar the journey. A couple of hairy types of hills were negotiated with apparent ease but little gullies where a bog seemed imminent had the two city folk a little apprehensive. Thomson took it all in his stride.

"Jus' two more hills an' a bit a' flat country, then we has a nice run t' th' creek wot runs into the Murrumbidgee up to th' north. It is at this 'ere creek wot me diggins is located."

Thomson grinned at the wondering pair.

"You must have a ride in my 'blitzbuggy' one day. It is much smoother to ride in than this four wheel drive." Justin ruefully noted.

"Golly, I do hope you know the way to get back!" Delumi said with a worried expression. "I have already been lost in the desert once and I do not wish to be lost again!"

Thomson laughed.

"Fear ain't a good companion. Yer won't git lost with me aroun', not in this 'ere stretch a' th' country. I been livin' 'ere all a' me life I 'as. Bin walkin' th' countryside fer yonks. I c'd fin' me way back 'ome blindfold I could."

"But what if you fall down a mineshaft or something we would never get out!"

Justin emphasised.

"See this 'ere little gadget. It's a compass. You just drive back due west and you'll come to th' road. If ya comes to a picnic ground, y've gone north too far. It's right on th' road. Jus' go south an' y'll come to your plane". Delumi felt a little better.

Soon Thomson stopped his vehicle on a ridge and they all went ahead on foot. We jus' gotta hike a bit t' them there trees an' walk along th' creek a bit." Thomson nodded with his head the direction in which they were to go. The two city folk had dressed in attire that they thought would be appropriate for slogging through the rough country. They were a little surprised at the ease with which the diggings were located.

"My word, we could have come here in our Sunday best. It is not very rough at all!" Delumi was at pains to comment.

“Heh, yez’ll be glad yer ain’t got on yer fancy duds when yez gits t’ diggin’. This ‘ere dusty dirt c’n fin’ it’s way inter y’ undershirt real easy!” Thomson chuckled. “Now this ‘ere’s where I located most a’ th’ gems. Yez c’n see where o’v shovelled th’ dirt, an’ that there is th’ ‘ole wot I dug down an’ foun’ that th’ place was lousy wiv them there sapphire things!”

“All right Justin, it is time we got a bit of dirt on us. May we fossick around a little?” Delumi asked of Thomson.

“Too right, ‘ere, o’l ‘elp ya!”

After an hour of scratching about in different spots two or three metres apart, Delumi was more than satisfied that indeed, Thomson had struck the jackpot. He showed the new chums the method of cleaning and separating the good stones from the rubbish by means of his couple of gold pans. Some of the sapphires were large enough to spot just by digging in this virgin soil – untouched by humans – possibly ever. Between the three of them, almost as many sapphires as those already obtained by Thomson; were recovered. Delumi opted to return to the shack and take stock of the bonanza, citing that it was getting dark and by the time they returned; it would be meal time again. They asked if Thomson would mind if they stayed overnight as taking off from the road in the darkness would be too hazardous. They were made welcome to stay as long as they desired. Weary but bubbling over with excitement, the three arrived back at the shack. Delumi was allowed first use of the tub to sponge herself down, (Thomson had no shower or bathroom in the shack) and while the men were taking their turns; Delumi busied herself with arranging the evening meal. The meat and vegetables were pre-cooked as Delumi did not know what cooking appliances were on hand. She had ordered a good supply from the canteen and had it packed in a portable ice-box. When Thomson came out clad in clean attire, he stopped and looked disbelievingly.

“Crikey! Where did all that come from?” He was amazed.

“Had it specially prepared in advance from my companies canteen.” Delumi obliged.

“Strewth. I ain’t ‘ad a meal like that in ages!”

"Well, stop drooling and sit down and enjoy." Justin urged, showing the way.

All sat and enjoyed the scrumptious spread. After they had eaten and the washing up done, not that there was much as Delumi had the foresight to bring a pack of paper plates, the three got to plan the next move.

"I will have Justin fly in two of our assayers when it can be arranged. While they are doing their thing perhaps Justin could look for a suitable paddock nearby. There must be a good spot in that valley or the previous one just over the hill from where we were fossicking, to make a temporary airstrip?" Delumi looked questioningly at Justin. Justin agreed.

"Yes, I looked around on the way back. There is an area that would make a possible landing ground for the Cessna. It is large enough but I will have to check there are no holes or big rocks that might bring an aircraft undone. When the assayers are doing their rounds I shall carefully walk over the spot and check for trouble."

"You could probably mark the spot out so you can judge the safety of it from the air!"

Delumi suggested.

"Yes. I will bring some white reflector domes and that will identify the patch I pick from the air." Justin agreed.

"So even on a dull day, you can still make them out?" Delumi asked.

"Sure thing that is one reason for white markers, coloured ones can be hard to distinguish from the rock formations, white stands out like a beacon."

Delumi turned to Thomson.

"I see that there is quite a hill out back of your shack. Is there any sort of view from up there?"

"Aw, too right there is. It is well worth the trek up to the summit. Ya know, it is jus' about th' best view around hereabouts. If ya looks to th' north, well, ya c'n see th' reservoir an' beyond. Whyncha two 'ave a look-see termorra 'fore yez fly out?"

Thomson asked with a knowing wink at Justin. Delumi failed to see this byplay. Justin reddened slightly and agreed that indeed, it would just about cap off the outing.

"Well, I am off to bed – er, where do I bunk?" Delumi queried.

Thomson showed her the second bedroom. It was cluttered with tools and men's paraphernalia but the bed was clean.

"You being the lady, can sleep in here. The young bloke can doss on the sofa in the dinin' room. 'Ere, o'l git some beddin'!"

Night descended and the trio slept.

Chapter Seventeen

ALL SYSTEMS GO!

Morning broke with a slight misty haze about the mountain top. Thomson was still sleeping peacefully when Delumi arose and after a quick sponge down at the water tank wash dish; went about setting the fire going in preparation for boiling the billy. Justin stirred at the movement in the kitchen. He too arose and after a sluice came fully awake.

"Good morning Del. I see you want a fire – here – let me do that!"

He took over and Delumi thankfully let him. She began making a toasting fork and some slices of bread ready.

"You do not need a fork for toast." Justin told her when he looked to see what she was doing.

"Well I am not going to get my fingers burned!" Was her reply.

"Why not just plug the electric toaster in?" Was the retort.

"Electric toaster?"

"Yes, I saw it on the shelf under the sink." Justin advised. "Oh of course, there must be electricity to the house; the light was on last night; silly me!"

Justin grinned and ordered a couple of slices for himself. Just then, Thomson went outside with his hair tousled and looking as if he was still asleep.

"Good morning." The pair chorused.

"Eh? Oh yeah, me too." He continued on his way.

They were sitting having tea and toast when a refreshed Thomson came into the kitchen. Noting that they were eating toast, he commented.

"Crikey, is they any bread left? I run out two days ago!"

"Oh sure, I will make you some nice toast and a cuppa. You just sit and talk with Justin while I prepare it!"

"Well, they is a mist on the mountain top again; should be a grouse day." Thomson commented. "Is you lot gunna go up that there mountin' like yez said ya would?"

"Oh yes. It looks like being a perfect day. The mountain is there, so is the view and we have all day to do it in!" Delumi said as she placed food and a drink in front of her host.

"When is you lot goin' back?" Thomson asked, a little apprehensively, Justin thought.

"Oh, I reckon we would stay for lunch before we leave. Just after lunch will be ideal for us; then we will get back to the office in time to make arrangements for the assayers. Do you mind if we ring tomorrow and make a definite time of arrival for my team to survey?"

Delumi smiled as she began clearing the few dishes.

"No, that'll be ripper; youse suit yerselves."

Justin and Delumi sat on a blanket gazing out upon the splendid vista of a haze covered valley. She leaned against his shoulder as she drank in its beauty.

"Oh Justin, is this not the most gorgeous place to be on a crisp clear day? I really do not want to go back to the polluted old cities."

"Mmmm." He just nodded, himself enjoying the moment. "You know -" He began "-I too would like to stay on here forever. You see, I have you to look at as well and you do so enhance a perfect setting!" Delumi pulled away and gazed deep into his eyes.

"Why, how sweet of you Justin!" She leaned over and gave him a peck upon the cheek.

"Oh!" Said a delighted companion. "Er – is that to be interpreted that we are on a holiday mode, or a business one?"

"Would it make any difference?" Delumi teased.

"Well you know how it is, you Boss, me Indian!"

Their eyes met and Delumi could see the love emanating from his heart. She took his face in her cupped palms and gently pulled him towards her glistening lips. They kissed passionately for a full minute. Justin separated from her face just enough to look her in the eyes.

"I really do love you Delumi – deeply!"

"Yes, I know and I you but just hang on to things a little longer and then when life is not so hectic – like when this change-over is complete; we may make lasting plans. Can you wait, my love?" His smiling eyes accompanied by a slight nod, was her answer.

The Cessna taxied along the road until it came to the prearranged spot selected by its pilot, for take-off. A hugely smiling Thomson sat on the fence-post waiting for it to pass. There was almost no breeze and the conditions could not be better for the aircraft to take to the air. At last the motor revved into full power and it began the short run it needed to be airborne. As they passed an excited Thomson, frantically waving, it gained altitude and after circling, began disappearing in the distance. Thomson finally climbed off the fence and made his way homeward, a little dejected now that his new-found acquaintances were gone. Still, their promise of a return soon had him lift his spirits and go about his business.

Delumi and Justin were back at their posts a good hour before their usual time of leaving the premises. Delumi got in touch with her assayers and after much deliberation, convinced them that to survey the area would not be a waste of time, although the two main people involved were pessimistic; Delumi was the person in charge and her word was law. A conference was set for the following day when all the details were to be thrashed out. She was beginning to look forwards to this meeting, for as promised, Thomson and his best interests had priority; the large sapphire on her desk was a reminder that he would be well covered legally. Promises to such a trusting man were paramount in her dealings with him and the integrity of the K.H.I.L. had to be considered. This little windfall, courtesy of Justin and his mishap, may not only pay for the aeroplane that had to be replaced but also she would see that Justin himself, was not to miss out on a share of the profits. After all; he need not have let on that the sapphires were available. A man of lesser standards could very well have taken a man like Thomson to the cleaners. Having had their meeting, and thrashed out a plan of action, arrangements were finalised for a contingent of top quality personnel to organize a sub-committee for the establishment of a wing of the K.H.I.L. to oversee the production of a mine workings, should one be needed. The two assayers and an assistant for Justin made the journey back to the shack of Thomson Geuring to verify that mining was appropriate. The two assayers were to stay at the diggings for a week to thoroughly explore the extent of the land to be mined. They took along supplies that would make them self-sufficient for the time. Justin would fly back in a week's time when their work was complete enough to initiate the selection. The area was to be properly pegged in accordance with regulations until such time as the land could be leased to the discoverer, Thomson Geuring; and then sub-let to K.H.I.L. for mining. To actually own the lease, K.H.I.L. was on a winner. Justin and his assistant dutifully mapped out a suitable airstrip for the Cessna and also a separate area for a helipad. Once the mine was up and running, both would be a necessity. There was barely one hundredweight of rocks to be moved and an old tree-trunk that seemed to have been there for decades, one rather uneven stretch where a hump was to be removed and a hollow filled; then Justin declared that the runway was adequate. Ten large round white reflectors along each side of the length of the runway were pegged down and a makeshift wind-sock laboriously securely tied high up in a lone pine which had seen better days, completed Justin's make-shift landing strip. When the time came for him to pick up the working party, they would not have that ten kilometre trip over virgin terrain to have to negotiate. A suitable helipad was located just by the screening trees of the small creek. In centuries past the assessors decided, a rather huge river flowed along the valley. Now just a trickle, it was hard to visualise a flood-raged torrent coming along the valley at all. Justin and his assistant, having set up the tent for the two assessors and packed their supplies away, bid adieu and made the return journey for the last time in Thomson's four-wheel. Once in the Cessna, they circled over the camp where the airstrip stood out once one knew it was there. On a whim, Justin tried it out. The landing was smooth and Justin taxied the plane back so as to be in the wind again, then straight away, took off and headed home. There would be a week to wait now so as the men on the ground could properly assess the merit of the diggings. Back at head office the paperwork was already being drawn up for a signature and all the proper and right wording was eagerly worked upon by the K.H.I.L. legal eagles to have a watertight agreement to present to the Government. One week later, when the initial exploratory work had been carried out; another extra-ordinary General Meeting was called for the immediate staff and some of the more influential members to attend. That a general meeting was called at all in an odd time slot was a matter of some concern. In this case however, a whisper doing the rounds of something big; had that privy to the whispers somewhat goggle-eyed. When Delumi took the chair for the commencement of the meeting, quiet enough to hear a pin drop permeated the hall. After the preliminaries were done away with, Delumi stood and faced her audience.

"Fellow members –" she began "- here–to– fore our business has been to invest other people's money. Klotz Holdings and Investments Limited have profited well by the shrewd and resourceful way our founder, Mister Thurston Klotz has conducted his business affairs. I have invited Missus Dulce Klotz to this unique gathering as I have something of great importance to share with you; and hopefully to get your full support on behalf of the K.H.I.L."

Delumi let that sink in before going on.

"You may recall that my pilot had a mishap a few weeks back and had to ditch the aircraft. We now have a replacement and we are back on track; not only with that but also with this upgrade move to the nation's capital. We are financially in a strong position; our Investments are way up (including the one that Thurston initiated in Western Australia) and now, since Justin's mishap. or rather because of it; we are now in a position to forge ahead even more. What I called this meeting together for is to gather your thoughts and approval for the K.H.I.L. to manage and operate our own mine. There will be no middle-man; the entire profits will be channelled through our company." She gazed about the silent audience and suddenly, dozens of hands were raised.

"Yes Tarwin?" Delumi pointed her pencil in the direction of the first to query her.

"You have had the mine assayed I presume but will it be a fizzer and all our profits dwindle away?"

"I have personally seen the diggings and I can assure you (based upon the assay reports) that we will be in for the long haul! Yes?" The pencil pointed again.

"Rumours are rife that it is not gold?"

"No Bob, this is a Sapphire mine and the assayers say it is loaded. We must at least break even at the worst but by all reports because of their quality, these Sapphires are top shelf!"

Such were the worries of the meeting. At its conclusion, all were in favour of the mine going ahead.

"Ah well, the stockholders are all for our move to go into mining and the Sydney move was successful, now we just have to wait and see if this mine delivers as promised!"

Delumi confided with Maureen, her secretary.

"Gosh! You do spring surprises on us out of the blue. At first I thought we had lost you in the desert, then to the movie world, now it is mining for Sapphires. Do you ever pine to live the sheltered type of life that everyone else aspires to?" Maureen asked with wide eyes.

Delumi just smiled. Then, after pondering the statement obliged with a somewhat cryptic remark that left Maureen even more puzzled.

"That could be closer than you think!"

"Huh?"

Said an unsatisfied secretary, as her employer quickly slipped out of the office on a personal errand, the errand took her to the canteen where she came across Justin having a coffee.

"Oh. What a pleasant surprise!" Delumi smiled.

“May I sit and coffee with you?” Justin grinned and asked. “One sugar or two?”

He went to the counter to acquire the necessary beverage.

“Need you ask?” Delumi chided.

“Force of habit!” He called back over his shoulder.

“So the meeting went as expected. You have your ratification?”

Justin plonked down after having placed a coffee in front of his boss.

“Yes, it was really a foregone conclusion but the membership must have their opinions aired!” Delumi sighed as she sipped the welcome drink.

“I thought Tarwin was going to cause some trouble when he was the first to ask questions. But it was just a mundane passing comment after all.”

“The assayers said it was a bigger field than at first visualised!” Justin remarked.

“Surprised me too, it just shows that one cannot judge a book by its cover. By all accounts, from what they confided to me, the pegging will have to encompass the whole valley. We will have to prepare for the future. Once we begin mining, the valley will have prospectors poring all over the place. We will have to set up boundaries so that there are no poachers. It does look to be more promising than even I imagined. Just as well I had the assayers come in and peg out a good cover. Oh! When next you speak to Thomson – no – the first thing tomorrow contact him and see that his personal mining right has been updated. This is most important. Will you see to it? If it is necessary, fly him in to the city and bring it up to date.” Delumi stressed the point.

“Sure, will do!” Justin responded.

When Justin duly contacted Thomson the following day, he found that the man had already been covered with an upgraded miner’s right earlier that year. His personal papers were in order and Delumi need not have been concerned; however, he thanked Justin on his astuteness and said that he was sorry it did not need upgrading as he would have enjoyed an aeroplane ride.

"Th' truth is -" he said "- I'd 'a loved to fly over th' area, I've bin walkin' th' countryside for years an' years; gee it 'ud be great to see the lay of th' land from a low-flyin' aircraft!"

He was put at ease on that matter. When next Justin was needed in the area (which would not be far away) a definite effort would be made to accommodate Thomson's wishes. The lonely old man hung up his telephone with a feeling of great anticipation for Justin's next visit. Delumi too, had thoughts of Justin on her mind. That he was in love with her she now knew for sure was not just a passing whim. Many of her acquaintances had shown amorous advances towards her but she had always been a little aloof. There were her share of wolves too; for instance that handsome Payne Carrens. But that the one stand-out love of her life was a person so near at hand, had almost been overlooked because he was an employee, an everyday acquaintance. Now, after a couple very tender moments with him, Delumi was more than sure he was the man for her. He had been ever the gentleman, had patiently bided his time and when the chances came for him, there was no 'bull at a gate' about him. He treated her with love and respect, almost with kid gloves, and when she asked him to be patient and wait until the time was right; that he did with grace and aplomb. Yes, he was a man worth waiting for, and the wait was becoming more and more unbearable for them both. Her secretary knocked and entered the room.

"Oh Delumi, this here memo you left - ?" Maureen noted the far away look in her boss's eyes.

"Er, I am not interrupting a clandestine moment am I?"

"Huh? Sorry Maureen, I was miles away. Now what is it you want?"

Delumi snapped out of her reverie and was immediately the person in charge again.

"You know – if I did not know better – I would have interpreted that melancholy look for pining over a lost love!" Maureen insisted.

"Oh piffle; I was just daydreaming is all. Now what is so important?"

Delumi tried to change the subject.

"This here memo you left – would not be a pilot would it - ?" Again Maureen fished.

"Could be – now what about the memo?"

"Is it getting serious?" Maureen insisted again.

"Maureen Dear, I will tell you in good time – now what about the memo?"

Maureen smiled a little knowingly but finished her enquiry.

"You wrote on the memo that you need me to write to Dulce Klotz. Er, just what do I write about?"

"Oh dear, I am so sorry. I knew so I naturally thought you did too. We must let Dulce know that the mining lease will not be in her husband's name, however Thurston's estate will share in it; the mine will be owned by Thomson Geuring but leased by K.H.I.L. Got that? I know you will draw up a draft that is worded correctly. Thanks Maureen.

As Maureen departed her office, Delumi added.

"At the moment Justin and I are just good friends. We have put anything else on hold until after this change-over is complete. Maureen!-"

"Yes?" The secretary popped her head back in the door.

"Do try and keep this just between you and I at the moment. I have no wish to embarrass Justin. After all, he is only an employee you know. If this knowledge gets to be public it could hurt him. Do be sensible and keep it quiet for now. Would you please?"

Delumi was at pains that it should be under wraps.

"Of course, you will let me know how it is going though."

"Yes Maureen, you will be the first!"

Chapter Eighteen

THE WEEK OFF.

A week had elapsed since the Sapphire Open Cut was inaugurated. Word had not got back from Government Departments regarding the leasing of the land; however work was well under way. Heavy machinery was being brought in and a useful road had to be formed from Currango Plains Road to the workings. A distance of some fifteen kilometres, the airstrip had been heavily used by Justin in ferrying in the workers and some light equipment. Even without Government approval, work was being done to have things in place for when official recognition was eventually granted. That seemed to be a foregone conclusion. It would be a great taxation boost for the people's coffers. Anything that brought income to the powers-that-be was rubber-stamped. Delumi stayed back at the office to see that everything that should be done; was done.

With the viability of the Sapphire mine doubling up on the work already initialized by Thurston at the gold mine in the outer reaches of Kalgoorlie, and both being over-seen by Delumi; her standing at the K.H.I.L. was concreted. That and the successful move to Sydney, the nation's capitol, had her high on the pedestal of authority as the prime mover of the company. Delumi contacted her second-in-command of the K.H.I.L. who used to be the Sydney Branch manager; Marcus Downes.

"Oh Marcus, how are things in your neck of the woods?" She cooed over the telephone.

"Hello Delumi, sure, they are going fine. What can I do for you?"

His cheery voice came back at her.

"Well it appears that the Open Cut is on schedule and the Sydney Offices are well established, so I thought it high time I wound down. If I take a week off, can you manage? Then when I come back you may have your own Annual Holidays."

Her query had the effect of boosting his by no means low morale.

"What a great idea. Of course that can be arranged. Have a wonderful time and it will be all systems go when you return!" Marcus assured her.

Delumi contacted Justin.

"Hello Justin. How is the work going at the diggings?"

"Ah, they reckon I am just about redundant now that the road is through. The workmen are established in portable home units now so I won't have to fly them in any more. Now I have the time to accommodate your every wish again. What is it, a trip to Kalgoorlie?"

Justin sounded as if time was running out for him.

"If that is where you want to go – well yes – but I had more in mind of taking a week off, sounds as if you could do with a week off too. Where would you like to go?"

Delumi awaited his answer with tongue-in-cheek. Justin was caught by surprise; he was quiet for a while thinking.

"Er – are you serious?" He was shocked.

"Yes, quite serious. We both need a break from our hectic lifestyle and a week off has been ordered!" Delumi was firm. Justin frowned into the telephone.

"Doctor's orders?" He asked.

"Yes. Doctor Vido has affirmed that this is to be so and we must obey the doctor's orders."

"Ripper-starting as of tomorrow?" Her young man was becoming enthusiastic.

"Call at my home about ten and I should have things all arranged by then!"

Two very happy young people were looking forwards to the coming week.

"Kalgoorlie sounds a bit far off and remote." Justin said the next morning as he waited while Delumi finished her packing.

"Yes and although it was nice at Thomson's mountain – or hill – we have been there constantly over the past few weeks. I crave for a new horizon!" Delumi sighed.

"Ayers Rock?" Justin suggested. Delumi shook her head.

"No, I could not bear the thought of bumping into that Payne Carrens again! Not that I would expect to find him there but memories of him and the rock are all bad. We even almost lost little

Jacinta there no, I wish to go somewhere entirely different!" Delumi was adamant.

"The Gold Coast?" Justin offered. Delumi looked at him, analysing the thought.

"Why not!"

They were winging their ways to Queensland on a clear summer's day, albeit towards the end of summer, and a week away from business made the two relax as they never had before. Delumi let her hand stray to Justin's upper leg and she squeezed it.

"Gosh I am looking to a great week off. No more board meetings or worries and with Marcus in charge I feel that I can let my hair down."

"Yes, I must say that I am feeling on top of the world now, too. Gosh Del, it was such a pleasant surprise – out of the blue – to find that I am on my way to the gold coast with you. What do you propose we do while we are there?" He glanced across to her.

Delumi just eased back in her seat and sighed.

"Just relax on the beach and if it is too hot – why – we will just have to loll in the air-conditioned lounge!"

Her pixie face smiled contentedly as she closed her eyes and feigned sleep.

"Ha!" Justin laughed. "Much relaxing you will do. Every two hours you will be ringing the company because you do not think they can perform without you!"

"Oh that is not fair. When I was lost in the desert for a week, they managed without me!" She pursed her lips. They continued the journey in silence; content with each other's company.

"Well it may not be Uluru where we are going but I can vouch that there will be a swimming pool. It so happens that I did not get to finish the demonstration of my diving prowess." Justin smugly informed.

"Quick – turn around – I don't want to see you embarrassed again!" Delumi exclaimed, in mock horror.

"You will keep. Come to think of it, I still have not drenched you as I promised myself I would do." Justin smiled.

"Ah – come on – let us call a truce and I promise I will behave."

Delumi leaned over and gave her man a peck on the cheek.

"Oh! Should I put it on Auto-pilot?" Justin grinned.

"Just you keep concentrating upon flying me to my holiday Justin. Time enough for fooling around when we are safe on the ground." Delumi firmly ordered.

"Sounds as if you don't want another Sapphire mine!" Justin pretended to grizzle.

"Heaven forbid! I am quite satisfied with the one we already have, thank you very much. Just get me safely to the gold coast!" Delumi once again settled back and relaxed.

"Oh! I had better ring through and have a vehicle awaiting us!" Delumi came alive.

She took a business card from her hand-bag and rang the hotel to which they had pre-arranged a booking. After a little conversation the private cab was ordered and it would be awaiting them at the airstrip some kilometres from the hotel. As the Cessna circled the strip awaiting the all-clear to land, the taxi could be seen standing by the control tower.

"Ah, lovely, it is good to know that money talks. When one has booked into the elite suite of a hotel, people turn over backwards to accommodate one!" Delumi gave a contented smile.

"Gosh. Talk about a spoiled little brat. I daresay you would have thrown a tantrum if it had not been there!" Justin teased.

"Oh tish and tash! Are you trying to throw a spanner into the works? I just may take the cab and let you walk for that!" Delumi wagged a finger at the pilot.

"And if I refuse to take you back?" Justin countered.

"Then I will just have to ground the Cessna!"

"Okay. I give in – truce!"

The polite driver was attending the door for his passengers when the light plane taxied over to the parking bay.

"Did you have a pleasant trip Madam – Sir?" He mechanically asked.

"Quite. Thank you!"

They were whisked away to the hotel. Upon entering the quite luxurious premises, an attendant assisted the driver with their luggage. The tired but excited pair was shown to the executive suite which had been made ready for them.

"Oh I just want to put my feet up and stretch out on that lounge there Justin. Wake me in time for dinner, there's a good fellow!" Delumi plonked herself down and closed her eyelids.

Justin grinned as he settled himself into an adjoining room.

"Good!" He exclaimed. "I have the choice of rooms seeing that you cannot be bothered. I will just pick out the one with the best view!"

Delumi was not to be distracted; she just dozed and let him have his way. At lunch, Justin casually glanced about the dining area in which they were sitting.

"Ah this is the way sensible people should always have their holidays. Nothing planned and a week to just idly while away. Amongst elegant people with their fads and fancies, beautiful sunny days and the lure of a pleasant after-lunch swim in the not over-crowded pool."

His eyes sparkled with enthusiasm.

"Now who is the spoiled brat?"

Delumi could not help herself, which was an opportunity not to be missed.

"Touche! I wonder if we will meet anyone we know?" He was still casually looking about as he said it.

“You would not know any of these people; they are too sophisticated for the likes of a crummy old pilot!” Delumi took delight in egging him on.

“Hey! Not so much of the ‘old’, crummy yes, but old – me – never!” He rose to the baiting.

“I though I saw Lennie just now – over there by that doorway.”

Delumi peered at the doorway in question.

“Rats. What would a cameraman be doing at a plush hotel like this one?” Justin quashed her remark. “You are letting your thoughts get away with reality. Just because we are in a hotel again; next you will be seeing Payne Carrens!”

Their lunch orders came and they immersed themselves with the fare.

“You know, after lunch why don’t we have a look about the shopping arcade. I really have not been on a shopping spree since that time at Central Australia. Do you fancy accompanying me on a stroll for an hour or so? Then when our lunch is settled, I just may be impressed enough to watch you skite – er – dive in the pool!”

Delumi grinned at the severe look she got from her escort.

“Just keep it up. I have a good memory and all will be paid back when I swamp you in the pool!” Justin played along with her.

“You were last one to ask for a truce. I do hope you are not going back on your word. There is no doubt about it – pilots cannot be trusted!”

Her accompanying smile caused Justin to grin himself. They got up to go shopping when who should walk up to them but Naomi Progue and Lennie, the cameraman.

“Delumi!” Naomi gushed. “Fancy meeting you here – how are you Justin?” She acknowledged her old acquaintances.

“I thought I saw Lennie before, are you on holidays too?” Delumi asked.

“Honeymoon!” Lennie piped up.

“Honeymoon?” Delumi was surprised.

Naomi held out her hand so that her wedding and engagement rings were visible.

"Oh they are gorgeous, you lucky girl. When did the knot get tied?" Delumi was all interest.

"Shortly after you fixed us up with those good jobs at the television studios, we had a nice engagement party then a month later, Lennie said to me - 'Why wait?' - and I said that we were wasting time, so we got married and here we are!"

Naomi received a peck on her cheek off her husband.

"She was so ravishing that I had to get her tied before someone else beat me to it!"

Lennie bragged.

"Oh I am so happy for you both. Are you staying here?" Delumi asked.

"Only for a couple of days, our budget won't allow much longer." Naomi grimaced.

"We are here for a week. Would you like to stay an extra couple of days – I will pick up the tab, call it a wedding present – oh do stay. I have so much catching up to do with you." She appealed to Lennie. "Make it an extra day or so for me Lennie. Go on, you owe me that!" Lennie looked at his new wife who nodded happily.

"Well, yes, we would love to!" They accepted the generous invitation.

"Good, now that is settled, Justin and I were going shopping for an hour and then a swim has been ordered. Are you two interested?"

"Well I am interested in the swim, but we have a little unfinished business to do first. Shall we meet at the pool in about an hour?" Naomi asked, with raised eyebrow.

"Fine, see you then and we can catch up." The two couples went their various ways.

Justin and Delumi were walking arm-in-arm along the shopping centre, both interested in the goods on display, when Delumi stopped by a bridal boutique.

"Oh Justin, just look at the beautiful gowns." His female companion drooled.

"Come on – let's move along." He brusquely attempted to drag her away.

"Oh! Justin. Typical man; I wish to at least admire them!"

"Yes, I know. I was just fooling; they are rather nice aren't they? But then, you do not need enhancing. To me – you are fine just the way you are – a jewel needs no other to prissy it up!" Justin gave her a peck on the cheek.

"How sweet, I am not so sure about this 'prissying it up' though." She squeezed his arm. "What sort of outfit should I wear? Do you like a tight bodice or how about a flowing gown with an extremely long train?" Delumi was fishing.

"Oy! Slow down. I may not even propose yet!"

Delumi thought this option over and then with a cattish smile asked.

"By the way; where would you like your ashes scattered?"

"Truce, I will submit to thee my beloved. You win; I do prefer the shortish gown with the firm bodice; if you must know!"

They continued through the shopping centre until an Antique Shop appeared.

"Let us browse through here, I love antiques!"

Delumi tugged her man through the doorway just in case he tried to bypass this shop.

"It is all right. I just happen to like antiques too."

The next quarter of an hour was spent looking with much interest at the old wares.

"You know Sweet; I think we should have at least one room dedicated entirely to the olde-world look. What say, is that how you feel?" Justin was in awe of some of the furniture.

"One room is no good. One either has a house full of antiques, or modern furniture. There is no half way!" Delumi informed.

"If ever I do get around to proposing, you may have the choice of furniture for our home!" Was the grandiose statement from her erstwhile companion? And a companion of old he was. Looking back over the years of employment at his current job, Justin wondered how it was that he had never been interested in another. Deep down he knew that from the first time he had clapped eyes upon Delumi, she was the one for him. He had bided his time and now it appeared that his every daydream was about to materialise.

Justin just knew he had won the fairest girl he could ever have dreamed of winning. Justin was more than contented. Delumi suddenly remembered her pledge to have a swim and they were to meet the newly-weds there.

"Come Justin, we must get back to the pool or Naomi and Lennie will think that we cannot be trusted to keep our word."

They hurried back and before long were entering the swimming complex. Lennie waved to them as they sat beside the pool at a table reserved for just such use. "There they are!" Delumi nodded the direction so as Justin could easily note at which particular spot in the pool their acquaintances were swimming. It being a rather warm day, there were plenty of people in the water cooling off. "Shall we join them?" Justin remarked, apparently not having his heart set on a swim. "Now do not tell me you are bored with it all, why we have but just got here?" Delumi chastened. "You stay out if that suits you – me – I am going to cool off." With that remark, she entered the water and swam with sure strokes up to where her friends were awaiting them. Justin belatedly decided he would join in after all. They all gathered at the edge of the pool, gossiping. After the initial excitement of the wedding was discussed and an exchange of likes and dislikes of wedding gowns were bandied, the past was the topic of conversation. "You know, as I said to Justin when we were deciding upon where to have a nice relaxing holiday. He suggested Kalgoorlie or Uluru but I desired somewhere absolutely different; so we thought the gold coast might just fit the bill. I needed to get away from the nitty-gritty of everyday problems. At Uluru we thought there were unpleasant memories – like when little Jacinta got lost and then that jolly 'L' character; you know, Payne Carrens. I believed we would have a holiday where we would be lost in the crowd – but guess what – we bumped into you two. I must say, it was nice though. And now you are married, well I can only wish you all the best and have a happy and fulfilled life." Delumi was so happy for her new acquaintances. "Sorry to spoil your fun but –" Lennie cut in "- the big bad wolf has made an appearance!"

All turned to see to whom he was referring. Payne Carrens escorting a lady sat by the table that Delumi and Justin had just left.

"Well I do not know about you people, me, I am going to swim to the deep end and maybe he will go away!"

Delumi said, not wishing that the Movie Director should know that she was at this holiday complex.

"You heard the lady!" Justin whispered. "Let us all go and perchance he will not bother us!" Justin accompanied his lady friend and as the pair of them swam away; Naomi and Lennie followed. They swam and frolicked about for a half of an hour, oblivious to the fact that an acquaintance was entertaining (no doubt) another movie star. Justin had only just got Delumi penned in a corner of the pool and with a hand on each of the walls at right angles to each other, smiled at his captive.

"Well now my lovely, it is about time I thought of giving you that ducking I promised!" Delumi eyed her man with the pitying look of a subdued animal, and then said.

"I wonder if Payne is still entertaining that lady."

"Huh?" Justin replied, looking around to see for himself.

While his attention was averted, Delumi sank and swam away. Justin glanced back to where he thought his quarry was still a captive, only to find she had gone. When he again saw Delumi she was with the others standing in the centre of the pool up to their necks and deep in discussion. Justin swam over.

"Well he is not there now." Naomi was saying.

"Perhaps they have left." Delumi hopefully suggested. "There is only one way to find out" Delumi pressed "and that is to leave the water and if he comes back, we will just have to put up with it! I for one have had enough swimming and I can think of nothing I would like more, than a nice fruit drink. Anyone else interested?"

The other three waded out of the water and accompanied her. They sat at the same table and waited for the steward. Their orders were taken and they furtively looked around, but no sign of the Movie Producer was to be seen. Evidently Payne was just passing through and by co-incidence, stopped off at the same hotel that the group of friends were staying at; Delumi hoped that was the case.

The next few days were a riot of laughter and good times had by the four friends. Delumi and Justin learned that Naomi and Lennie were both extremely happy with their new connections in the world of television. Their work load was heavy but fulfilling and there was not the same pressure put on them by their employers as had been the scenario at Uluru. The payments were good and their work was very interesting.

"We can not thank you enough for pushing us in the right direction!"

Naomi was at pains to thank her benefactor.

"Did you know that Justin and I have delved into sapphire mining?"

Delumi asked, by way of changing the subject, a little embarrassed at being reminded of it all the time.

"Sapphires?" Lennie exclaimed.

"How interesting!" Naomi was perplexed. "How on earth did that come about?"

"It was really Justin who came up with it. When he ditched his aircraft in that reservoir, the chap who came to his aid just happened to be a gold prospector. He stumbled across the sapphires and had Justin help him out with marketing. It looks like being a goer!"

"How very exciting!" Naomi gushed.

"Yes. The Company is mining it for the owner and we have a tight hold on the lease. We hope to have an easy time of things now, what with that and the gold mine in the west, to say nothing of all our other leases; the K.H.I.L. is swinging along easy street nowadays!" Delumi smiled a contented smile as of a pampered old pet. "Plus we have moved head office to Sydney that should make international contacts easier to manage."

"Gosh, what a lucky pair we are, Lennie and I, to even be on speaking terms with Managing Director of such importance." Naomi blinked.

"Goodness me –" Delumi chided "- you make me sound like some sort of a demi-god, which I am not. Just you treat me like one of your good friends – nothing more – else I will not treat you both to dinner this evening!"

"D-dinner?" Lennie came alive.

"Yes. After all, I did invite you for an extra couple of days. I do not expect you would have budgeted for them. I believe we should dine away from the complex for a change. Any suggestions?" Delumi grinned at the perplexed looks she got from both her friends.

"What a great idea, you have surprised me Lennie. Where on earth did you come up with the idea of a night out at the fun-fair?"

Delumi blushed and attempted to cool her hot cheeks down as they alighted from the scenic railway and made for an ice cream parlour.

"Oh, I guess it is just the boy in me, I do not think I ever quite grew up!" He laughed. "It was fun though, especially when that sudden drop almost straight down seemed to come from nowhere; your scream nearly broke my eardrums."

"Yes, and mine." Naomi added.

"Chicken feed. You lot have been too coddled that is your trouble – how about the 'Climax' now?" Justin suggested.

"Oh no, leave me out. I have had my fill thank you; I think we had better go over to the restaurant now that I have worked up an appetite. Are we agreed?"

Delumi checked with the others and when they concurred, all set out and crossed the road. The nice evening meal had the four friends leaning back with a cup of coffee to settle the food down.

"Oh dear, it is back to the grind tomorrow. But what a glorious time we have had, it was much better having another couple to share it with, I am so glad that we bumped into you two!" Delumi said and meant it.

"Gosh, it was a god-send for us; we could not have afforded to have such a good time on our meagre budget. Thank you so much. Oh, by the way, you said you have moved the main office to Sydney. Does that mean you will be moving there too?" Naomi asked.

Her wide eyes begged an answer.

"Yes. I am afraid so. Of course every now and again I will be commuting back to Adelaide for a few days; we may bump into each other again. Anyway, I will give you my new 'phone number and you can always call me!"

The accompanying smile made Naomi feel that she would not lose contact with her new friend so easily.

Justin breezed into the office after his first day back at work. There were a few urgent packages to transport and the aircraft needed a going over for its monthly warranty check-up, however, not a great deal was on the books for the rest of the week. He mentioned as much to his employer.

"You have just had a week off; I hope this is not leading to more time off!"

Delumi had an expectant air about her, as if pre-empting what was on her pilot's mind.

"No, of course not, however something has to be settled."

Justin watched Delumi's reaction carefully.

"Hello, what have you been up to?" Her furrowed brow gave just a hint of worry.

"You know how you love to dance?"

"Yes?"

"Next Saturday evening there is to be an annual get-to-gether of the employees and their families at the town hall. It will be the first one at this new venue for the company since our move to Sydney."

"Yes?" Warily came from Delumi.

"May I ask that you accompany me to that event?" Justin was all agog with eagerness.

"Well I was about to have a quiet evening at home --!"

"Then you will come – good, I will pick you up at eight!" Justin hurriedly made his exit.

After he left, Delumi mused to herself.

"Now what is he up to I wonder?"

It was a night of still air and quiet moonlight that beckoned quite a large crowd in to the local Town Hall. The throng of people all laughing and talking made a hum of interest and activity that verged on a carnival atmosphere. Into this crush Justin escorted his young lady with all the aplomb and brashness of youth. The lower hall was where the refreshment tables and make-shift bar were temporarily housed. Justin ushered his ladylove to a secluded quiet corner (well almost) where there was a fair chance that they would be able to converse more easily. They were constantly accosted by this couple or that who wished to congratulate Delumi on the way she had run the affairs of the company. Stockholders as well as Staff had been invited; therefore the hall was heavily attended.

"Would you like something to whet your whistle?"

Justin asked, and then left Delumi alone while he acquired the refreshments. He arrived back and had to stand waiting while Delumi spoke with more friends and acquaintances. Eventually they realised they were in the way and departed. Justin offered Delumi the light wine which she had ordered. The young couple sat out the preliminary dances until the more energetic younger people had worn themselves down somewhat, conversing of things that interested them both; Just enjoying their own company. When the dances commenced, many of her admirers let themselves become caught up with the activities. Delumi began looking to the dance floor so Justin got up and offered his arm to Delumi. She accepted and they became lost in the whirling throng on the dance floor. After a half an hour of gyrating around, they headed back to the table where they had left their tops, discreetly guarding the places they had chosen.

"Oh that was lovely Justin. You have not lost your charm on the dance floor. Reminded me of the fun times we had at The Red Centre."

"Yes and no 'L' to move in on me Justin playfully added.

"Oh, that reminds me. I wish to apologise for running off with him and leaving you in the lurch but I just needed to know if he was a flirt. Anyway, I did get even with the big lug and through it all Naomi got rid of him too. It was well worth while!"

"Would you care to walk with me out into the quiet of the hallway, I have something that I wish to share with you?" Justin eagerly asked.

"Ooh, that sounds serious. Come on then, I could do without the crowd and the noise for a few minutes!" Delumi led the way.

They stood silhouetted in a large bay window with the full moon shining upon Delumi's hair, giving her a somewhat ghostly appearance.

"You know I really do enjoy these outings with you. I know the trip to Thomson's hill and the times we spent there were great. The many times we have travelled together in the Cessna and that week away up at The Gold Coast with Lennie and Naomi; ah, I did not want to go home." Justin was really wound up which caused Delumi to ask.

"You are leading up to something, what is on your mind?" She cautiously asked.

"My word you do look ravishing in the moonlight."

Justin took her hand gently in his own and kissed it, and then dropping to his knees took a small box from his pocket and offered it to Delumi.

"I have waited until I can not wait any longer – Delumi – marry me. Please say yes!"

He peered at her with a worried look; expectantly. Delumi opened the box and a gorgeous diamond engagement ring sparkled back at her. With a stifled gasp, she stood spellbound, staring at her engagement ring. Justin was still upon his knees. Delumi with a tear rolling down her cheek eased him to a standing position.

"Please Delumi; I love you so much it hurts. Please say yes!" Delumi nodded.

"Yes. Oh yes Justin. It – it was so unexpected. I mean it was not unexpected I always knew we would marry – but – I, I thought it would be awhile yet – I? Yes Justin, yes, I would love to spend the rest of my days with you!"

The two were engrossed with kissing and hugging for which there was no need of words.

THE END